Is It
Good for
the Jews?

Is It Good for the Jews?

MORE STORIES FROM
THE OLD COUNTRY
AND THE NEW

Adam Biro

Translated by Catherine Tihanyi

THE UNIVERSITY OF CHICAGO PRESS
CHICAGO AND LONDON

ADAM BIRO is founder of the Parisian art book publishing house Biro Éditeur. He is the author of nine previous books, including *Two Jews on a Train* and *One Must Also Be Hungarian*, also published by the University of Chicago Press. CATHERINE TIHANYI is a translator and research associate in the Anthropology Department at Western Washington University.

The University of Chicago Press, Chicago 60637
The University of Chicago Press, Ltd., London
© 2009 by The University of Chicago
All rights reserved. Published 2009
Printed in the United States of America

17 16 15 14 13 12 11 10 09   1 2 3 4 5
ISBN-13: 978-0-226-05217-5 (cloth)
ISBN-10: 0-226-05217-6 (cloth)

Biro, Adam.
[Marchand de lunettes et mes autres histoires juives. English]
Is it good for the Jews? : more stories from the old country and the new / Adam Biro ; translated by Catherine Tihanyi.
    p. cm.
Sequel to "Two Jews on a train".
ISBN-13: 978-0-226-05217-5 (cloth : alk. paper)
ISBN-10: 0-226-05217-6 (cloth : alk. paper) 1. Jews—Social life and customs—Fiction. 2. Jews—Social life and customs—Humor. I. Tihanyi, Catherine. II. Title.
PQ2662.I733M3713 2009
843'.914—dc22   2009020092

♾ The paper used in this publication meets the minimum requirements of the American National Standard for Information Sciences—Permanence of Paper for Printed Library Materials, ANSI Z39.48–1992.

CONTENTS

PREFACE

In an earlier book, *Two Jews on a Train*, I attempted to invent stories, to tell short stories based on jokes whose endings are known to everyone, that is to all lovers of Jewish stories.

This idea appears to have been appreciated, so I am repeating it here with other stories.

However, this new book differs from the preceding one. Here, I'm not so much concerned with telling jokes, but—please forgive my lack of humbleness—with creating literature. I am also aiming at giving more depth to my short stories, making them relevant to the present, politicizing, uncovering their links to the *grande Histoire*, to a mostly recent history, but to an older one as well.

Moreover, for this new volume, I did read scholarly and semischolarly works, analyses, and books, including even the Talmud, partly in order to find inspiration in the very roots of Jewish humor and partly to understand its mechanism, its whys and wherefores.

I came to the tentative, unavoidably tentative, conclusion that Jewish stories don't have specific principles and structures. They resemble every people's stories, yet at the same time, because the "heroes" are Jews, there is no other writing that can translate or better narrate their soul, history, millennial suffering, their few joys—there's nothing more revelatory of the Jewish being.[1]

PARIS, JULY 2008

---

1. In contrast to all of the books I read, I will not provide any explanation of the orthography of Hebrew and Yiddish words. I am following no rule except that of usage and my needs.

[Some of the orthography of common Hebrew and Jewish words has become part of the English language; thus I am following established practice wherever it is indicated. — TRANS.]

TRANSLATOR'S ACKNOWLEDGMENTS

My thanks to Adam Biro for tirelessly answering my questions and for kindly reading the translation and making further suggestions. In the process he also made some changes from the original French. My thanks also to T. David Brent for entrusting me with this translation and to Paul Stoller for reading it and contributing some fine suggestions. Last but not least, my thanks to Carol F. Saller for her excellent copyediting of this book.

Is It
Good for
the Jews?

*   *
    1
*   *
    *

In Lieu of an Epigraph

A BRIEF STORY CONTAINING WITHIN
ITSELF ALL THE FOLLOWING ONES

Two Jews meet in Budapest on Dob Street during bad times, during one of those very many bad times when you had to tremble, to fear for your family, your possessions, your work, your life (in this order). This might have been in 1899, or in 1920, or in 1944, or in 2007 . . . or again during the Middle Ages when Jews were expelled from Hungary (and from France, and from Great Britain . . .)—except that Dob Street didn't yet exist.

They were of course called Kohn and Grün.

Why "of course"? If you were a Hungarian Jew, if you were lucky enough to be Jewish and Hungarian—and these according to my father are the most precious jewels in the crown of Creation, an opinion that I am not far from sharing—you would not be asking this question. And if you are neither Jew nor Hungarian, is it really worth my while to give you an answer? In any case you wouldn't understand it. But I'll make an attempt anyway: Kohn and Grün, two Hungarian Jews, are Mutt and Jeff's cousins, Laurel and Hardy's soul brothers.

So:

Kohn whispers to Grün: "Did you hear that twin sea lions were born in the Oslo zoo?" (For a member of the People of the Book, and the reading and writing this entails, it would be more logical to ask "Have you read?" And yet, the exchange of words of mouth might be the last remaining bit of warmth, the last human link remaining in our troubled world. Since when? Always. The use of the conditional mood here, of "might," is only for the benefit of grammatical convention.)

Grün moves close to Kohn and, worried, whispers into his ear: "No, I didn't hear about it. Say, Kohn, is this good for us?"

The Officer's Ring

In contrast to many of the stories whose origin I am ignorant of, this one has a clear identity. It was told to me around 1910 by my friend Molnár Ferenc, the unforgettable author of the most beautiful novel in the world dealing with youth, The Guys of Paul Street, and who later was to make his living as a scriptwriter in Hollywood. (Scriptwriter in Hollywood! My dream and that of all Hungarians.... It's a bit late, you might tell me. Hungarians are getting pretty scarce in Hollywood. But remember the sign posted on the door of one of MGM's studios: "It's not enough to be Hungarian to make movies; one also needs talent." Robert Capa came up with a variant: "It's not enough to have talent to make movies, one must also be Hungarian.")

This story happened in the "good ole ancient Hungary," that of "before Trianon,"[2] a topic apt to provide a subject for conversations lasting evening long to any Hungarian, discussions livened up by *barackpálinka*, that is apricot brandy, and by *expreszó* made with Hungarian-style burnt coffee.

Eh, I'm thinking as I'm talking to you that I will put this story at the very beginning of my book. It sets the decor: that of Central Europe for folks nostalgic for the old Austro-Hungarian empire, and, for politically conscious folks, that of Eastern Europe, that is, the countries occupied after World War II by the Soviet Union. These are geographical notions devoid of any relationship to geography, but having lots

2. The Trianon treaty, signed at the end of World War I by Hungary and the Entente countries ("imposed" would be a better word than "signed," as the Hungarian delegates were not even admitted into the negotiation room), redrew the borders of Hungary, which thus lost two thirds of its territory.

to do with politics, history, psychology, literature, writers, readers, émigrés, the indifferent, the elected, not to forget the nonelected and the self-elected, as well as diplomats of all stripes. . . . These are confused notions. Should some of my stories lean toward the West (oh, this troubled word, this two-faced carrier of dreams, this noble louse of a word!), toward for instance France or the USA, this would be a sign of a desperate attempt at assimilation. But this first story isn't running such a risk. The characters are clearly defined: the Jew will be very Jewish; the goy will be a devil of a goy.

So, let's get back on track, as I did get a bit lost here. I'm doing it on purpose. I find getting sidetracked delicious. "My style and my spirit are both wanderers," said my friend Montaigne, my best friend. My anecdotes are thus pretexts. Pretexts used to remember, to think, to speak aside, to wink—pretexts to wander.

This story thus happened in the "before Trianon" Hungary, the "good ole ancient Hungary." (No correction, please; "good old" is an idiomatic expression reserved for holders of senior cards on French trains, while "ancient" should be pronounced with a sigh and a slightly shaky voice. And always welcomed is a gaze slipping upward—to Upthere?). Thus I'm not the best one to speak of the "good ole ancient." While that Hungary was indeed old, it was not good; it was stupid, and criminal to minorities and Jews. I might be more inclined toward discussing the "before Trianon." Indeed, few countries can boast of losing two thirds of their territory in the span of a couple of days. The Trianon Treaty imposed on Hungarians by people whose hatred was equal to their ignorance was more than a folly; it was a mistake. The Hungarian right doesn't need any other food: it has eaten, burped, and farted Trianon for more than eighty years and is still unable to swallow and digest it.

So let's forget Trianon. It's all right for us Jews to forget it, because we have been "bad Hungarians" for the past thousand years. Yes, we did live there and still are, between the Danube and the Tisza; we've been there for a thousand years, even before the Khazars converted to Judaism. (Bad Hungarians? Bad whatever you wish: bad French, bad Germans . . . bad Jews even.) They, the true bloods, the "seasoned vets," are good. The only good ones. They have come up with all sorts of good reasons to make a meal out of the Jew, the Tzigane, the Romanian, the Slovak, the Croat (am I forgetting someone?), since Trianon and before Trianon.

Oh well, let it be. After all, aren't we here for a bit of laughter?

Thus: on the right side of this greater Hungary, in Transylvania, which is today Romania, lived a pious Jewish usurer, pious and usurer, pious but usurer, usurer but pious. (It's me speaking here. It's me adding these scornful "buts." You might well tell me: we all have to make a living. I know Jews—rabbis' sons—who make a living, and a good one, from debt collecting, who own all sorts of agencies, who are financial brokers. . . . I despise them a little, the collection agents, the credit brokers. Whether or not they are Jewish, it's the same to me. This doesn't mean that they are despicable *hic et nunc*; it means that they are despicable in absolute terms, in relation to what I believe to be ethical, to rules of behavior that are not only Jewish but simply human. "The world has been abandoned to men's care." It's Graham Greene who wrote this, as the good Catholic he was. In the hands of those people, the debt collectors, the credit brokers, *oi vei tsorres*, the result is telling. At this stage of my life and my thoughts, with the encounters I have unfortunately experienced, I no longer need to be careful. I can say whatever comes to mind before it descends into the heart and then, even lower, into the iBook, so that my dislikes are always well grounded).

This usurer belonged to my family. In Transylvania, on my mother's side . . . or my father's (who can tell? All of my folks came from Transylvania). I hesitated admitting this. After all I just said about debt collectors and credit brokers. . . . Eh, you have to make a living. This usurer has been an old story from the time, oh God, my family passed to the other side. Alas, the side of the plundered, the victims of *recollectors and debrokers*.[3] So some ill-gotten gains would have come in handy. My father hated business, despised money, and reproached me for being a publisher. "You're *selling* books in Paris!" What an insult! And when he died at age ninety-six there wasn't a cent left in his apartment in Budapest, *not one cent!* I am italicizing it. Nada, zero. And

3. [This is an attempt to recreate in English an equivalent but of necessity different play on words to that invented by the author. The original French reads *intercouvreurs et de remédiaires*, playing on *recouvreurs* ("debt collectors") and *intermédiaires* ("brokers"). — TRANS.]

it was the same at his bank, give or take a few bucks. Not even enough to pay for his funeral. And, truth be told, this pleased me. And I'll do likewise; I'm already doing it.

In another corner of Hungary, all the way in the upper-right corner that was called in Hungarian Felvidék, the Upper Region, and which is now called Slovakia, in a garrison, a well-born officer was officiating. Soldiers are often stupid; even though the empire had two heads, its officers remained microcephalic. Their stupidity outdid the average circulating in the northern hemisphere. Scornful, xenophobic, anti-Semitic (and also antiminority, all of them), nationalists (every man for himself, for his own nationality), arrogant, ignorant, lazy— and lousy soldiers to boot, losing all the good wars that came their way. Our officer was different from the rest. Oh, not by much. He wasn't a genius. And yet . . . And since our story happens during the Belle Epoque, a forty-year span of peace, he didn't have anything to do. Thus he indulged in skirt chasing (more often skirts that didn't require much chasing, which could be lifted or taken off in a jiffy at the clinging sound of money) and he gambled. Let's call him Szentlajoskúty Bódorogi Arisztid. It's a name from the old country. His fellows in the regiment called him Ali. We'll follow their example, happy to not be forced to use this name that is a bit too goy, a bit too long. (I know French equivalents. And when I say equivalents . . . what do you think of Marie-Anne de Montboissier-Beaufort-Canillac or of Hugues-Aristophane Galissart de Marignac? And what about Joseph-Louis-Amour Mis de Bouillé de Chabrol, or again, Jean Cornand de la Crose? I'm not making them up, honest!)

Ali was a card player like all the other officers. We shouldn't confuse card games with chess. Cards require neither intelligence, nor abstract thinking, nor a sense of strategy. (Except bridge, so I'm told. But were they playing bridge at that time in the Upper Region?) Cards demand neither humor, nor culture, nor physical strength, nor character, nor beauty of body or soul—they demand almost nothing. It's enough to know the rules of the game and have a bit of memory. The rest is left to chance. This is the way they were killing time (oh God, our time has already such a short life . . . how could one want to kill it?). I think that Ali, even though his intelligence was above that authorized by headquarters, didn't know how to do anything else, except also play the peacock in front of women. . . . I assume he knew how to court them as was the practice in those milieus. You had to be well spoken. Of course after this, if unfortunately the prize let herself be dragged to bed, you had to be up for it. Up what? Up the bed. It wasn't expected (not yet) for a man to pleasure women. The sexual pleasure (rapid, much too rapid) of his Highness the Officer was enough. An honest woman did not feel pleasure. After that you got married and went back to seek your pleasure in the cards.

I said that Szentlajoskúty Bódorogi Arisztid was well born. This means that his parents were nobles. Small nobles, members of the moneyless gentry. Nothing more. To be well born involved neither wealth, nor diploma, nor gumption, nor beauty, nor intelligence, nor any of the things I enumerated above. It was enough to make the effort to be born in the right place.

As for the Jew—we'll call him Salomon—we don't have much good to say about him either. What do you expect? He was a usurer. Did you really think that I would say good things about a pawnbroker, a *collecting recreditor*? Even if he was a Jew, even if he was a member of my family? (Yes, I know, I know, money was our profession because we were forbidden any other. Still he could have practiced another of the professions allowed Jews: victim, or musician, or rabbi, or philosopher, or writer or . . . stop! What am I demanding here? It is easy to reproach others to not be geniuses. So I speak to myself, author-narrator bent on amusing his readers, what have you done with your youth? Remember Rimbaud, Mozart, Van Gogh? And Evariste Gallois, the greatest French mathematician of all time, dead at age twenty-one? So, how old are you, you sermonizer?)

And while Ali had a certain style, an allure provided, formed by the uniform, Salomon had none; he was nondescript. And he was not even wealthy. True, he was well-off. However, he had many children—how many? Who knows? Did he know himself, what with the stillborn, and the others dead in infancy, and those who went away to seek their fortune to Budapest, the capital, or in America? Thus with all those children, money kept on disappearing and disappearing.

Salomon had known Ali for a long time. He had often rescued him (we are speaking of money, of course) when his regiment was stationed in his town. They say they even succeeded in conversing with each other, I mean in a human manner, about people, the weather—perhaps even about politics? A certain feeling of friendship was born between them. You don't believe me, because you have read too much. Not only was Ali not stupid, but also he had heart and courage. Both of these were needed in those days and at that place to speak to a Jew as a human being.

At the time the famous exploits that I am about to tell you occurred, the Sire of Szentlajoskút's[4] regiment was garrisoned, as I mentioned, quite far from the town where Salomon lived, he who never had moved in his life. One day, Salomon received by mail a small package to which was appended an urgent letter from the officer. There were no polite formulas, no convoluted introductory phrases, no complicated circumlocutions. No, the letter was brief and direct: "Dear Friend (note that he calls a Jew a friend!), I suffered gambling losses, it's a debt of honor, I don't have a *pengő* left. I'm enclosing my golden ring. I urgently need 200 *pengős* by return mail. However, this time not a *fillér* less; it has to be exactly 200. If you can't or don't want to, send me back the ring (which is worth much more)—but I absolutely refuse any negotiation. Yours, etc. P.S. This ring bearing our arms has been handed down in our family from father to eldest son for generations. So you can see the sacrifice I'm making by selling it."

Sacrifice—how dare you speak of sacrifice, you miscreant. Aren't you ashamed? You gamble your money away and you waste what is the most precious in your family. . . . Salomon was not in charge of the young Szentlajoskúty's ethics or of the salvation of his soul. So sensing a good deal, he didn't lose any time in replying to the officer. "Dear, etc., your ring is worthless. [Here the storyteller simplifies. Salomon's style was much more flowery. While he was in a hurry, the deal was not as urgent for him as it was for the officer. So he composed carefully, used all the proper formulas and as much space as he fancied.] It's not even 18 carat gold, and its form, its style are completely out of style, without it being old enough to be an antique. It is thus impossible to resell it. I am still your friend but not crazy. I have a wife and children

4. The terminal Hungarian *y* is the equivalent of the French particle *de* ("of") indicating nobility. I am skipping it here; otherwise it could be read as "of of" (*de de*).

dependent on me. I don't have the right, if only for their sake, to indulge in blunders. I should thus return your ring immediately with this letter. However, I sensed while reading your letter that you have a genuine problem and are in real trouble. In the light of our long-standing friendship and the quasi-fatherly feelings I have for you, I cannot bear to only listen to my head. At times we also need to listen to our heart. This is what I am doing by offering you 50 *pengös*. And not one cent more. This ring is worth zero *pengö*. Zero is what I would get from this deal, because I won't even try to resell it. Nevertheless . . . etc. Send me your agreement, and I will immediately cable you the money. Your Devoted, etc . . ."

The reply quickly arrived. "Salomon, send me back the ring immediately. I said 200. I need 200. Not 50, not 60, not 199 but 200. Will you stop, at least for this highly important deal, this insufferable haggling of which your people has made its profession and which is so hard on the Hungarian noble. [So! Anti-Semitism in the form of presumably harmless small everyday utterances was only awaiting the opportunity to show the tip of its disgusting ear!] I thus await 200 *pengös* or the ring. Yours, . . ." No etc.

Salomon did not rush to his quill. Let him stew a little, the sire officer, my anti-Semitic friend. "Your people," I could tell you a thing or two about "your people." After three days—in the meanwhile he had to respect the Sabbat—he proposed for the sake of the ties between him and the Sire of . . . and *von und zu*, with a *y* at the end, and all his ascendants, and of whom he already knew the father whom he had as well helped on numerous occasions, and because he couldn't abandon a friend in need, and yada yada yada (this later is said differently in Hungarian, but the meaning is the same) and etc. and re-etc, so ok, 80, that is my last word, my last figure, my last proposition, my last offer, my last gift, or I sent you back the yada yada.

"No, and no," replied the officer, whose more and more unreadable writing showed his impatience and anger. "200, 200, I said 200! Stop your *pilpul*! Send me back the ring." (So all of a sudden we have become very familiar?)[5]

5. [In French, as in Hungarian and other languages, there is a familiar "you" (*tu* in French), which the soldier uses here, and a more formal one (*vous* in French). — TRANS.]

Well, this is not going to happen this way, says Salomon to himself. He wrote a long, extremely, excessively polite letter. No mention of "your people" nor of the *pilpul*, nor of the familiar mode. No, it was a highly sensitive letter, emphasizing the lack of value of the ring, the cluttering caused by this useless object, and, to speak the truth, not a very attractive one at that, in the moneylender's home, who, given his ties yada yada would never dare yada yada throw it away (because any resale was inconceivable). As to wearing it, he didn't even dare contemplate such a thing, being himself just a Jewish moneylender without any sort of pedigree and not deserving to compare himself to the valorous Magyar nobility, and bla bla bla and more yada yada yada, in short, 100. "And always devoted to your wishes, I remain your humble, etc." Pretty polite, no?

"Jew, enough—send my 200 *pengös* or return the ring immediately." The mask had gone. They were back in the Middle Ages. The pyre was already built on which Jews were burnt for having poisoned wells or spread the black plague. This can happen very fast. Have you heard of a certain Captain Dreyfus? France came close to civil war simply on account of a little blue list!

Salomon was holding tight. The more Ali was losing his nerve and his civilized veneer, the more Salomon kept on expressing his friendship, the concern he felt as he read the increasingly "anguished" (Salomon's word) letters from Sir Officer who could be his son, who *was* his son. He was begging him not to take drastic action (150, last offer), to think, he was so young (170, that's all), that he should consider the immense, the absurd effort his old friend was making on his behalf fearing that the young man would hurt himself, by offering him 180 *pengös* (one hundred and eighty, have I gone mad?) for a bit of metal devoid of beauty and value.

In reply to his last letter, cutting, angry, filled with swear words, swirling with insults and negatives, Szentlajoskúty Bódorogi Arisztid received a small package. Inside, there was another, smaller package accompanied by a letter. I'll spare the reader the declarations of friendship, the description of the pain suffered by the author of the letter, that felt by the humble Jewish moneylender Salomon, who himself suffered as he imagined the situation of his lifelong friend, and then at the end : "If I offer you here 190 *pengös* it's only because of our re-friendship-pain-never-always-still. If you accept, then do not even bother opening the package containing your ring. Just sent it back to me immediately, my address is already written on it, and the money will be sent by return mail. If your youth and your lack of experience prevent you from accepting my ultimate offer, then, too bad, just keep your ring and we will not speak of this matter again. Never again. Don't ask me anything else. We no longer know each other."

Military Ali was no longer thinking. In a rage, in fury, he pulled out his pocket knife and with one motion cut off the cord tied around the package, and tore the wrapping paper carefully folded over the box.

Inside, instead of the ring, he found a note scribbled by Salomon: "OK for 200."

In Praise of Anti-Semites

I am wondering if it wasn't Doctor Andrée P., who, one day on the phone, first told me the witz that follows. I say witz purposely because my friend Andrée, in spite of her Polish family name, Pi, comes from North Africa and her maiden name is in reality Pe. Yiddish is thus not really her native language, the shtetl isn't her point of origin, nor can she brag about belonging to the great creative Hollywood family. This hasn't prevented us from being friends for the last thirty-seven years.

Two Jews are seated at a café. Where? Anywhere—the story that follows is universal. You'll see. So let's make our life easier and locate it in a place that I am very familiar with, that you would be interested in knowing if it isn't already the case, and that I can visualize while telling the story, since it's where I'm living: Paris, France (warning to readers from Versailles, Illinois, or Dublin, California: not to be confused with Paris, Texas, or Paris, Louisiana). I'm speaking here of the City of Lights, that of the Declaration of the Rights of Man (World War II: seventy-five thousand Jews picked up by French police all over France and then deported to the camps by the Germans . . .)

On the sidewalk section of a Parisian café, the two Jews are seated in the sun, during this famous and celebrated springtime sun that only Paris can produce. As to Parisian cafés, I would tell and retell you about them if it hadn't been already done and redone and re-redone. I am like everybody else, *glücklich wie Gott in Frankreich*, happy as God in France, happy as a lark, in love with Paris, with the cafés, with lovers. . . . But you might tell me that the French are anti-Semites, because you're thinking only of *that* all the time, even in Paris, you who have the ex-tra-or-dinary luck to live in *this* city. It's true, but not for all of them, and they are not *just* that. And then: they are no more anti-Semitic than, unfortunately, I am assuming, all the other nations in the world. I'm choosing my words carefully here: I do mean all the peoples, without exception. In Japan, where there are no Jews, there is apparently an organization of anti-Semites. There are barely ten thousand Jews left in Poland, which boasts of an anti-Semitic party, anti-Semitic priests, and anti-Semitic ministers of state.

I don't know if you're like me (what a hypocritical question, because everywhere and always, you're only thinking about *that*): seated as I am in the sun, in a Parisian café, with hopefully a bit of a breeze, I'm already halfway on the road (to happiness, I mean). And, if perchance a friend, and particularly a woman friend, is keeping me company, then there is not much missing for me to say: I was right to come down here (on this earth, I mean).

And yet, our two fellows were not happy. Happiness requires a predisposition for it. Albert Camus used to say that he was gifted at happiness. It's a gift: you either have it or you don't. Our two Jews didn't have it, it was evident; it was engraved on their foreheads. Among other things because they were only thinking about *that*.

One of them, Moïse Fogelseher, is sipping a decaffeinated coffee (it has a chemical taste—but one must be careful with one's nerves, not to mention insomnia!); the other, Shlomo Talesschmutzer, is enjoying a bottle of Vichy Saint-Yorre water (disgusting—excellent, according to Doctor Zizesbeisser, against uremia, which leads to gout, which, in turn inevitably ends up triggering kidney colic, which, if untreated or not properly treated, lead terrifyingly to death). After swallowing their foul-tasting drinks, they each pull out a newspaper from their pockets. Moïse disappears behind a rag sheet published (undercover, as it is illegal) by the extremest of a violently anti-Semitic extreme-right faction. Shlomo is reading *Ha'aretz*—in Hebrew. They look at each other. Moïse is surprised by what Shlomo is reading.

"What! You're living in Paris, you speak French, you vote in France, and you're reading an Israeli daily? I didn't even know you could read modern Hebrew. I never heard you speak *ivrit*. Aren't you a bit snobbish? You don't even know what is happening around you, in the next street, but you're interested in Tel-Aviv news."

"I know only too well what's happening in the next street. They are burning synagogues, they are drawing swastikas on the walls, so what can I say?"

"They, who?"

"Them. In *Ha'aretz*, at least I'm reading news about Jews, about people like me."

"So why are you living here? Why don't you go live in Israel with people like you? You should be more consistent."

"I am consistent. I'm French and I live in France. Isn't this clear? And you, show me what you're reading. What? I must be hallucinating! You're reading *La France aux Français* [France for the French]? Am I seeing right? This rag that I wouldn't even want to touch with my hands for fear I couldn't wash out the filth afterward? That's what you're reading, you who are reproaching me for reading a Jewish paper? I knew you were a bit *meschüge*; now I believe that you've become totally nuts. I swear you should be locked up!"

Moïse looks calmly at Shlomo, lets him huff, bang on the table, and jump up and down on his seat before answering him: "Not only I'm reading *La France aux Français* every week, but I have subscribed to it."

Shlomo jumps up. "I'm leaving. I'll never see you again. You're no longer my friend, I don't ever want to speak to you again. I refuse to be friends with a subscriber to *La France aux Français*. A paper that wishes for our death, our disappearance, that misses Nazi times, that denies the existence of the gas chambers even while stating that too many Jews came back from the camps. And this is what you're reading. And besides, you're giving them money. You know what happened to my family. I don't wish to remind you of my history. Nor of yours, which you seem to have completely forgotten. Farewell!"

Moïse grabs Shlomo by the sleeve.

"Don't leave—let me explain."

"There's nothing to explain. It's quite clear. You've become insane; you're dangerous. Unless you've become a fascist. It has happened, fascist Jews. You always had weird ideas. You were always weird. I was often warned against you. I was told you were not quite straightforward. I wasn't listening to gossip. In fact you're very straightforward. You're a Nazi. I don't want to see you again."

"All right, but before breaking up our friendship forever, listen to me for five minutes. Five, that's all I'm asking. Five minutes against forever. After that, do what you want."

Beside himself, Shlomo sits down again. "It's a mistake to listen to you, but since we'll never see each other again, I don't want . . . "

"OK, show me your Israeli daily. Let's see the front page. You can read Hebrew but I can't, so would you please read me the headlines?"

Shlomo grudgingly does as he's asked. He pulls out the paper from his pocket, carefully unfolds it, and gently with a sort of reverence lays it out on the café table and translates. "Here, on top, is the main headline: '16 people dead during an attack against a bus in Jerusalem.' It's horrible. Can you imagine, and in the meanwhile, while our people are getting massacred, Monsieur is reading *La France aux . . .*"

Moïse interrupts him. "Yes it's horrible. You need incredibly steady nerves to be able to live there. Every day, or almost every day, there's an attack. Keep going. Let's see the other headlines."

"Down the page a bit: 'Unemployment went up 3% in Israel. The most recent statistics . . . '"

Moïse interrupts him again. "No, just the titles. Otherwise we'll never finish, and before we're through, you'll leave forever as you announced. I asked for five minutes, so keep going. Let's hear the other headlines."

"Next to this: 'Israel's brain drain is increasing. Forty university professors have left for the United States since the beginning of the year.'"

Moïse laughs. "Not bad."

"What do you mean not bad? No, really, I don't want to have anything to do with you."

"You promised me five minutes. So read more, on page two."

"Here the whole page is taken up with an in-depth article dealing with the deterioration of Israel's image in the world and its consequences for the Jews of the diaspora."

Moïse laughs again, even more than before. "Excellent, keep going."

"Anti-Semitic acts are increasing in Europe."

Moïse: "No comment, and on page three?"

"That's the page on the economy. You want it?"

"Of course, keep going."

"Inflation in our country has reached . . ."

"I'm lapping it up. Keep going. What's on that page?"

"It's the sports page. I don't think you're interested in it."

Moïse gesticulates with impatience. "Of course, I'm as interested as can be! I'm interested in everything that has to do with Israel! Of course."

Shlomo slowly turns the page and reads: "The Maccabees lost 3 to 2 against the Lithuanian team of . . ."

Moïse can't stand it anymore. He's ecstatic. "Against a Lithuanian team. Beaten by the Lithuanians, on top of everything!"

Then suddenly he calms down. He repositions himself comfortably in his bistro chair and says to Shlomo that if he ever had doubts or scruples reading *La France aux Français*, his scruples have now disappeared and he can see how right he has been. He abruptly opens up his weekly on the table in the place of *Ha'aretz*, which he sweeps away with the back of his hand, greatly upsetting Shlomo, who rushes to retrieve it and refolds it carefully.

"Okay," continues Moïse. "Let see. I don't need to translate, since you read French as well as I do. Since we are both French, from birth even! So, look at the first page, the editorial. Its headline is 'Jewish France.' I'll summarize it for you; I've already read it: France is in the hands of the Jews. The president of the republic, the government, the economy, all of the state bureaucracy—in short a monstrous international Jewish conspiracy—is dominating France. Then just pick any headline below and read it."

Shlomo, disgusted, turns his head away. "I told you you are crazy. You read this and it makes you happy? They have been speaking about this Jewish-Masonic conspiracy for over a century. It's over a century ago that Drumont's book was published with the title *Jewish France* and it provoked scuffles, the breaking of store windows, old people roughed up, hate demonstrations all over France. . . . And you're rejoicing! You bastard. I'm calling you a bastard, a fat pig. Forget me. Cross my name and address off your address book and even off your memory."

"One moment, Just give me one more moment; the five minutes are not over yet. Look at the headlines: 'Michel Rosenberg just bought our fellow paper *Le Clairon du Bas-Lochois.*' And here: 'We're learning that the new owner of the movie theaters chain 'Q-culture' is called Ariel Baumzweig. No need for comments.' Then there's a long article of literary criticism on the last winner of the Anastase prize, Jean Martin. We read in it that one of the great-great grandfathers of this Martin came from Poland and was called Kohn, and this explains his intellectual approach and his style. Can you imagine the time and the energy spent on all this research? Moving on, 'Behind Bush is the Jewish Texan community which is controlling 30% of Krumply oil company.' In short, my dear Shlomo, if you read this paper carefully, you'll discover that we the Jews, we own all the films and movie theaters in the world, all of the good corporations. We are in the background or a part of each government, we're controlling the Nobel Prize jury, we dominate the academy, we are in charge of publishing and music companies, we are responsible for the bankruptcy of a certain corporation, because it brings us profits, and also of the success of another one for the same reason. . . . I am reading that we are the kings of the universe, that we are the wealthiest, that we decide war and peace. We have the most beautiful women, everything we touch turns to gold, we are never sick, we live to a very old age, and we succeed at everything— moreover, we are infinitely happy! So I have to tell you, I love this paper. It fills me with happiness and pride to be Jewish. While your newspaper of misfortune, your *Ha'aretz,* what does it tell us? It writes about unemployment, attacks, deaths, poverty, inflation, brain drain, defeats—and all this happens only to Jews. So, you can understand that if I have to chose between reading one of the two . . ."

4

Of Humility

This joke was told to me by Larry B. But because of his origins, Larry set it in his home territory, that is, in a New York taxi, with two young Yankee rabbis, modern, elegant, and proper, and a Black Haitian taxi driver. As for me, I prefer to locate it in the "old country," where I'm on familiar grounds, and where one of the two rabbis was certainly a member of my own family.

Bundled up in a pile of ancient patched blankets, two old Galician rabbis were seated on the benches of a horse-drawn uncovered wagon on its way toward the ancient city of Tarnopol. That is, when it was still called Tarnopol, when Jews were still living in it, many Jews even. (In addition to people, men, and women, the Second World War destroyed a culture, a language, a literature, a music, culinary practices, modes of dressing, customs . . . let us not be afraid of a big word: a civilization. This is rarely spoken about. Jews, *Gott sei dank*, still exist—there will always be Jews—but that Jewish civilization of Central and Eastern Europe, that of Lemberg and Tarnopol, of Mád, and of Kisujszálás, and others, many others—the list is endless—where not one Jew remains, that civilization has been irremediably wiped off the map. And, in spite of the desire I feel within my own self, I'll never forgive and will keep on tirelessly repeating to those Jews and non-Jews who feel it's time to turn the page that this forgetting is a horrible thing to contemplate.)

It's cold, as terribly cold as the weather could be at that time and in those countries. (Galicia, have you heard about it? No, it's not the Galicia in Spain—it's one of those many improbable countries, one of those provinces far away from the sea, continental, with a conti-

nental climate: hot in summer, cold in winter. These are provinces
with adventure-comics-type names of which the Austro-Hungarian
empire and Eastern Europe held the secret. Examples, in no set order,
are Bukovina, Bessarabia, Ruthenia, Transnistria, Banat, Vojvodina,
Transylvania, Moldavia—have you heard of those places? All right,
enough word torture. I too am ignorant of all the African peoples, all
the states in the United States.)

Everything is frozen around them, everything is white, but it is a
cold white. There is no snow. The silence is oppressive; the only sounds
would have been that of winter noises, the wagon wheels crunching
on the frosted-frozen road, and the old horse's regular trotting, if it
weren't for the constant talking by our two clergymen. As to the driver
seated up front, it is hard to make out his human form, so much is he
buried under numerous layers of jackets, coats, blankets, and thick
silence. But the two, seated at the back of the wagon, are speaking
nonstop. This so as not to give in to sleep in spite of the temptation
in this great cold. And also because they have things to say to each
other. They see each other rarely, even though their villages are next
to each other. And then: they like to talk. They are wordy folks. Wordy,
so they talk of everything, of the life of their respective communities:
marriages, deaths, births. In this order. Marriage is one of the most
sacred duties, death strikes people they know, and births can be left for
the end, since they have to do with beings that they cannot yet know,
who, in their eyes, don't have any existence yet. Then they broach
other events: the harvest, natural catastrophes, accidents, strange,
supernatural happenings that occurred in their villages. Dead coming
back to haunt the sleep of the living, livestock refusing to let themselves be killed, prayer books bursting into flames when opened, Old
Rebecca who spat gold. . . . They also talk about money, of their all too
meager income, of their large families. A bit of the country's politics,
but not too much—they are not really informed. And they don't wish
to be. They either refuse to know about technical innovations or are
not interested in them. Polemics about ideas are not their polemics,
because they are not their ideas. They don't read newspapers—news
can take days, weeks, before getting to them, and that is when they do
reach their hidden shtetls. They live a life that is *elsewhere*, a life out-

side the country they are living in. They speak another language—Yiddish—they dress differently, they eat other types of food, they have other customs. And they do have another religion. Of course, even though they have their own rabbinical tribunals, they are subject to the laws of state. They pay taxes and are required to serve many years in the military. But they are still elsewhere. They're still awaiting the Messiah so as to finally return home, to Jerusalem.

The rabbis also talk about their relations with the goyim, the neighboring peasants. There is lack of understanding, mutual mistrust, hatred, often violence. The Jews despise these Ruthenian Galicians, uneducated Poles, pork eaters, crude drunkards, while the peasants hate the Hasidic Jews who killed Our Lord Jesus Christ, Jews whom they see as arrogant, and who, they assume, are hiding enormous wealth in their homes, and whose clean and mysterious daughters they lust after. Mainly, the Jews are foreigners, incomprehensible—in short, aliens. People not like us: no other explanations needed.

After exhausting all of their repertory, the rabbis move on to religious matters. They are learned, they know the Torah very well, they have studied the Talmud all of their lives. It's a game, but it's not just a game. This peeling away, this cutting into parts, this meticulous examination of letters, numbers, words, phrases in ideas point to the deep yearning dwelling in every Jew, that is, the desire to understand the world. The only submission should be to God, and the rest can be dominated through understanding and intelligence. It suffices to read the Talmud to make out the Jewish underlying desire to grasp the secrets of the universe, a refusal to accept the absurd and the incomprehensible. Tertullian wrote: *Credo quia absurdum*, "You must believe because it is absurd." The most poetical, desperate Christianity allows for this. As for us, when faced with the absurd, we have the need to seek what lies behind it.

"You know, in truth, all that, all this vain agitation, all these people and their problems, all this village bore me," says the older one. "I'm only interested in study. I am wasting my time when I am not reading books, when I'm not pondering a phrase or a word in the Torah. It's the only thing I'm supposed to do on this earth. Reading, studying, trying to understand what the Eternal is asking of me . . ."

The other, younger though barely so (both rabbis are well into their seventies), interrupts him: "I find you pretty pretentious. To understand the Eternal? Do you realize what you're saying? Yes, you must study, but don't expect to understand a thing. You have to study because it's your duty. If at the end of your life you succeed in understanding even the first letter of a line that God has dictated to Moses, well, then you could say you haven't lived for nothing. As for me, I know that I'll never understand anything, that is, in the real sense of understanding. I remember rules, methods, my duties . . . but understand? Never."

The older one answers that his colleague has not truly grasped the sense of his statement. He doesn't have the insolence to claim to understand the paths of the Creator. He isn't even trying. He is content to just try to get an understanding of God's orders, to grasp what He is asking of him. "What is my role? In the village? Courage is required to even read. Fear seizes me each time I open a book. Who am I to dare reflect on the *mitzvot*, the commandments? Who gave me permission to even reflect? Doesn't reflecting imply weighing the pros and cons? To doubt? As if there could be, as if there were pros and cons! I feel that I am absolutely nothing. What am I saying 'I feel'? I know! I have barely the right to open one eye. In the hands of the Very Holy One, I'm but dust."

"Dust, you say? Pretentious, still pretentious, arrogance! Me, I feel that I don't even have the value of dust in God's eye. I am nothing, simply nothing. In the infinite universe ruled by God, I don't exist. My life doesn't even last a second, my existence is of no account, what I do, what I think carry no weight. No, my dear Shmuel, I am nothing, that's all." And the rabbi forcefully repeats: "I-am-no-thing."

The older one gets agitated. "To be nothing is yet too much. It means that you believe you *are*. But *are* you, in the eye of the King of the Universe? To be nothing, that's still a claim. Me, I feel that I am less than nothing. I am an absence, a hole, a void in the face of our Creator. Simply, I *am not*. And this doesn't make me sad, on the contrary."

At that point the cart driver who has not said one word since the beginning of the trip, curled up as he was in front of the horse's dancing behind, turns around toward the two rabbis even while still keeping a firm grip on the reins. "I've been listening to you. You're saying that you're nothing. You, well-born rabbis, rich, learned, intelligent, cultured, well fed and fat. Nothing at all. So what am I to say, me, poor miserable cart driver, without any education? If you're nothing, you two, then I am worth even less than you. I am the nothing below the nothings."

He has barely finished speaking than one of the rabbis, turning toward his colleague, exclaims indignantly: "The nothing below the nothings? Who does he think he is!"

* * *

A Yiddish saying perfectly sums up this story: Mach dich nicht asoi klan—di bist nix asoi gross. *"Don't make yourself so small—you're not that big!"*

5

Okuláré

The last lines of this joke are hidden in a very old Hungarian book, Seiffen-steiner Salamon adomái, published in Budapest by the newspaper Borsszem Jankó ("Johnny Peppercorn") in 1920. The word adoma, meaning "anecdote," is not very Hungarian and might have a Greek or Latin origin. As to the two other words in the title, if you can't understand them, it's because Hungarian is truly a very difficult language.

My father was an oculist or ophthalmologist, depending whether you are a Latinist or Hellenist. And if you are neither because your school-ing stopped at *Dick and Jane*, I'd tell you that he was an eye doctor, not to be confused with "optician," who is basically an eye mechanic.

I have written and spoken at length about my father in my books and to people. And also with myself, while walking in the street, at times in an elevator, while looking in the mirror, or in the morning while shaving. I am astounded. I resemble him to a startling degree. There's a poor-quality Polaroid taken by chance during a family meal . . . hal-lucinating: seated side by side, my father, who was eighty-six, and I, fifty at the time, both holding the spoon in the right hand, the left arm leaning on the table, around the plate. . . . We are perfectly parallel, like two stereoscopic images. The way we are holding our heads, the hands holding the spoon the same way, at the same height, the left arm, the bend of the body . . . and the identical expressions on both faces, con-centrating on the soup, and showing indifference, and acceptance . . .

When I read the following story, that of the eyeglasses, it made me think of my father. He loved jokes, he told them often, and he would repeat his favorite jokes to whomever was willing to listen, particularly to me—an excellent public, simple and naive for anything that is tale or story. I love stories whether they be fantastic, horrible, smutty, salacious, or simply funny—I love them all. And the more slapstick they are, the more I laugh, as I am fond of cream-pie-in-the-face gags, of Charlie Chaplin and Laurel and Hardy. (The jokes my ophthalmologist father told were always very proper).

I think he would have appreciated the one I'm telling you here, first because it has to do with his profession, which he loved above all else (yes, above all else), and then because it's a very old story, coming from the distant beginnings of a century luckily forgotten, the twentieth, so that this tale would have satisfied my father's taste for the past. He was born in 1905 (unavoidable parenthesis: unfortunately the horrible twentieth century cannot be forgotten, but if the twenty-first keeps its promises and keeps on going along its initial trajectory, it is bound to best it—good grief!).

I would like to talk about our friend Grün.

(When I think of all the things that have happened to these two fellows, Kohn and Grün, these essential actors in the great Hungarian Jewish tragicomedy! And they are still enduring! You might remember that I presented them to you at the beginning of the book.) Kohn *bácsi*, generic Uncle Kohn, Old Kohn—strangely, they never said Grün *bácsi*. They are going to be and are at times cowards, at times—though rarely—daring, at times believers, and at times—so few—miscreants, as well as stupid and brilliant, at times—most of the time—both honest and dishonest, faithful and unfaithful. . . . And if you were to tell me that they sum up the human species, I would tell you no. They are only the representatives of Central European Jews. And I'll not get involved in the argument pitting the supporters of "Eastern" against those of "Central"—I'm speaking of Europe, of course. You surely get it. And what if the "East" in "Eastern Europe" came to be seen as a promise instead of the dangerous blight it is now? Beware: in one hundred, in fifty years, Metternich's insulting statement "Asia begins at Landstrasse" will be taken as a compliment![6]

Our friend Grün is selling eyeglasses and magnifying glasses,

6. The Landstrasse is today located in the center of Vienna, but in the nineteenth century it was at the easternmost limit of the city.

which, at the time of our story, were identical. Particularly in the countryside. The peasants who were getting old became weak, could no longer hear, and weren't able to see very well. To see what? TV didn't exist. They didn't read. But for wealthy peasants and the provincial bourgeoisie, things were different. So they were wearing magnifying glasses, eyeglasses, *ókuláré*, as they said in Hungarian one hundred, or rather one hundred and fifty, years ago. Or again they were called *pápaszem*, pope's eyes—popes were wearing glasses.

Grün thus makes the rounds of the bicephalous empire, on foot, and at times by train. Sometimes a cart driver feels sorry for him and offers him the depths of his cart filled with warm hay. There, listless, Grün contemplates like a child the sky while holding tight against his chest his leather suitcase with the precious eyeglasses, his living. Upon arriving, he extracts himself stiffly from the cart under the laughing gaze of the driver, who has no good reason to help him. Back on his feet, he tries in vain to pick off the straws sticking to his coat.

What Grün really likes are markets, fairs. He sets his suitcase on a stand, opens it, and has passersby try his specs. Women come to him just to see themselves in the mirror, to see something new adorning their face, while only the men are buying. Grün owns an elegant hand-held mirror that he holds up in front of the client; it is just big enough to house a pair of glasses and a nose and at the same time small enough for the buyer not to be frightened by the grotesque image of his whole face.

So in a fair, he can make as much as he does during two weeks of door-to-door selling.

Door to door . . . that's his cross, if we can use this Christian expression for a practicing Jew who stops all selling activities during the Sabbat and holy days. His cross, that is, his *ókuláré* case, he has to drag from village to village, in addition to the sack containing his *sidour* (prayer book), a chunk of bread, an onion, and a few spare underwear and socks. (*Fuszekli*, my grandmother used to call socks, a distant and improbable deformation of a nonexistent Germanic expression *fuss-sack* and of its Austrian diminutive, *fuss-säckli*, "foot purse"). Running away from dogs as mean as the peasants who, drunk or sober, rain blows and insults on him, call him "dirty Jew," drinking apricot brandy at the time of payment, or instead of it, coming close to drowning in the torrential rains of the great continental summer, and when his clothes are dry (because they have to be dry before meeting a client), being covered from his hat to his shoes by the sand of the great plain of the Carpates basin, keeping one eye open while sleeping in dangerous inns, selling to the men, courting the women, joking with the children—all this to sell? For money? No way! To live. To give a meaning to ALL THIS, on earth.

It is in this state of mind that Grün arrives at Kohn's house, a wealthy wheat merchant. He's not expected and not welcomed. Kohn has worries. Summer in the Hungarian *puszta* has been catastrophic; there was not enough rain and thus the harvest has been dismal. He's had a bad year. At the moment when Grün, covered with dust and exhausted, comes into the house with the beautiful covered porch, Kohn is in the process of doing his accounts. Precisely. Just at that moment. And since he is neither precise nor correct, he is stressed out. Everything stresses him out. The least noise, contradiction, wasp, mosquito. And there are plenty of mosquitoes, wasps, and even hornets, and so many contradictions in this place. Kohn absolutely does not wish to see Grün, who sends him a return message with the servant saying that if Kohn doesn't want to see him, very soon he'll not be able to see anybody or anything, and particularly not his money. "Tell your master that if he wants to see, he has to see me. Repeat my words exactly. You'll repeat them, right?"

So a furious Kohn stomps out of his office. "Who is this stupid jokester? Ah, it's this *schnorrer* Grün again? So what are you selling now? Because I've have to tell you the glasses you sold me . . . let me see . . .

Grün interrupts him. "Five years."

"Five years? I see that you have lost your memory, my poor fellow. It was last year!" But Grün is too smart to start his visit with an argument that would only add to Kohn's negative feelings toward him. "Yes, certainly. So what's wrong with my glasses, I mean your glasses, Mister Kohn?"

"What's wrong? Nothing, actually, nothing. That's the whole problem. You sold me window glass. I cannot see with or without those eyeglasses." Grün shyly mentions that time has taken its toll, even if it has only been one year (five! exclaims Kohn—three, responds Grün) and that, with due respect, while the magnification power of those glasses has not increased—how could it—Mister Kohn's sight must have deteriorated.

Kohn doesn't want to hear it. He rejects Grün's point with a flip of his hand. "You fooled me. You sold me a good-looking frame with worthless lenses," he tells him. And you, you *ganef*, you dare come back ..."

"I hear you, Mister Kohn," replies Grün. "That's why it's time to help you. You need to be able to see. With your responsibilities, your lands and wealth, your obligations and functions in the county and the synagogue, you must be able to keep an eye on everything. And a good one, one equipped with a good lens. Just try this one." And he pulls an *ókuláré* in a metallic golden frame out of his suitcase, a case that once upon a time, a long time ago, was new. He adjusts it on Kohn's big rubicund nose.

"It's not better than before" says Kohn.

"And this one?"

"Neither," and so on. Grün changes the frames, pulls out lorgnettes, pince-nez, monocles, more glasses in silver or golden metal, in steel, in genuine tortoise shell (from South America, says Grün). It's slow going. Grün is aware of this; he is used to it. He keeps on changing one frame for another, all with identical lenses. Just like in the theater, it's a change of sets in full view of spectators. He pretends to chose the lenses carefully and scrupulously; he takes a long time painstakingly studying the small print description next to each one. He frowns and puts on reflexive airs. Then, after trying on the sixth pair of glasses, Kohn feels he's had enough and has other things to do. When Grün, seated facing Kohn, puts the last glasses on his patient's nose, this latter first shuts both eyes, then blinks, then opens them wide and says: "These glasses are fine! But ... but ... tell me, Grün, what is it that I'm seeing? A crook!"

Grün keeps his cool. He looks surprised as he carefully takes off the glasses from Kohn's face. "Really?" he says. "Do you mind?" He puts them on himself, adjusts them, looks at Kohn in the eyes for a long moment, and suddenly exclaims: "My goodness, Mister Kohn, it's true! You're so right!"

6

Of Wisdom

I read or heard this one . . . I don't know where. . . . Our paths must have crossed. It must have lingered at the same places I did. It is deep, believe me. It illustrates a sentence from the Talmud: Khol akava letova, *that is, "Each obstacle is for our own good." But I have to confess that, as far as I know, there was never a rabbi in my family. A day laborer, yes, and also a member of parliament, a university professor, an ultraorthodox pipe maker . . . but no rabbi.*

Three rabbis were in the habit of meeting about once or twice per month to drink two or three glasses of vodka and then walk around for one or two hours in the two or three hills surrounding the town they were living in.

Where did they live? As far as I can remember it was neither in Lapland nor in Ladakh. Someone in the audience might well ask me: why not? Are there no longer any Jews in Lapland or in Ladakh? My answer is: yes. They are/were everywhere. It's a question of proportion and probability. At one time in the history of Europe, it was known that there were more Jews in Lithuania than in Lapland. As to Ladakh . . . oh well. Thus let us say that this story could happen any place where there is (1) a town, (2) two hills, (3) Jews, (4) three rabbis. (And some vodka of course. However, having learned that to be accepted in Mongolia, you have to know how to ride on horseback, sing, . . . and drink vodka, I have to conclude that it is drunk everywhere.)

Jews must talk. The Talmud advises us to be mistrustful of the tightlipped as well as of the windbag. (Just as it also warns about the arrogant, and the overly humble, another form of arrogance. Which thus makes the story "On Humility" a Talmudic one).

To read, study, reflect, discuss, argue. Confrontation and contradiction give birth to new ideas and modify or elaborate old ones. They bring us closer to the understanding of the world—the one goal we Jews pursue all our life, and have sought throughout our history. (Is it necessary to add that this understanding is completely illusory? The more we believe we are understanding, the less we understand. The more we believe we are coming closer to the Goal, the more it withdraws. However, let's not complicate things here). These rabbis who are deep in a discussion—that's banal! When they aren't studying, they are discussing. In both cases, they are trying to understand the world.

The three in question always take the same path for their walk, and this for the last twenty years. They know it by heart; they know every tree, every turn, every bit of ascent, every slope. "Knowing" is not quite the right way of putting it. They know only the itinerary. They must absolutely not change the route. It is particularly important to keep to the same trajectory so that the newness of the path, its unusual attractions, its surprises, its beauty or ugliness cannot capture the holy men's gaze and distract them from the discussion of ideas. Once the itinerary is set, fixed, recorded, and memorized, they no longer see anything: flowers blooming and then fading away, enormous trees toppling over from old age, new buds, mushrooms, falling leaves. . . . They ignore the freshly plowed fields as much as the gold of the wheat ready to be harvested. They don't notice changes in the landscape or in the colors of the sky. They are barely aware of the sun, the rain, and the snow. They don't even see themselves: ideas, the thread of reasoning, have taken them over completely, their eyes, their ears, all of their body, and their mind.

One day, the tenth day of the tenth month, a torrential rain flooded the place. The inhabitants were very familiar with rain. It was a rainy country—but no one had ever seen such a rain, never. You couldn't see anything. The water formed a heavy curtain. Thick-skinned animals with the sensitivity of, well, beasts, sought shelter. The shadows, the outlines of trees that could barely be guessed at through the wall of water, became fantastical, menacing. That day, the rabbis were forced to renounce their walk. They didn't have cell phones; they didn't have phones period. Or maybe the phone didn't exist yet—can you imagine? It's true, so how did Montaigne communicate with his friend La Boétie? And Eloise with Abélard? And if the Portuguese nun and Madame de Sévigné wrote all those letters, it was because there was no more juice left in their cell phones for texting. The three rabbis knew each other well. They were each aware that the walk was of course canceled, put back for later, but for when?

As soon as the rain stopped, the oldest one put on his clothes (his everyday clothes of course—rabbis in the olden days did not wear sweats), and he went to the colleague who lived the nearest. The third rabbi was already there, and they left together in the air cleaned and purified by the rain. The sky was a deep blue, cloudless. Everything was new. The storm was barely a memory. The three rabbis set out on their ritual perambulation. They looked at the sky, so clear, and wondered about the weather and its changes, about temperature, also. If the weather were uniform, could wheat grow? If it didn't grow, and neither did barley and oats, what would people and animals eat? However, one of the rabbis noted that in some other places the weather never changes. In Africa it is always hot and in northern regions it is always cold, and the sky is constantly blue—or gray—and people and animals are still fed. So they concluded that the Saint, blessed be His Name, makes wheat grow in countries where the weather is always changing, and in other regions, he makes other plants grow that are suited to the ambient climate. And if He doesn't make anything grow, as in the desert, it's because people are not supposed to live there. But if they took a chance and went there anyway, God, blessed be His Name, could in His mercy send them rain or manna, like He did for our ancestors in the Sinai. One more time, they were in wonder of the infinite wisdom and forethought of the Creator who doesn't leave anything to chance. And if a torrential rain falls on us, the Lord knows precisely why. And if this rain causes damages, destroys the harvest, floods the fields? And if lighting hits the head of a family on the road? Here again, it's all ordered, planned, calculated. And how should men react? Do they have the right to go against the actions of the Eternal, replant the wheat, dry the swamps? Of course, because it is said that since they were born, they are obligated to live. They thus must feed themselves. And the man hit by lightening? Will he come back to life? No, of course not, but his widow will marry, as is the custom, one of the unmarried brothers of the dead man. And if men are under the impression that God acts against their immediate interest, they are forgetting that God's paths cannot be understood, that the aims of the Eternal are impenetrable—and that His actions are only in the interests of men even if they cannot understand Him. And if the traveler hit by lightening is young, it's because his premature death serves a divine purpose. The clear proof that God is all-powerful is that He can do anything, and that man must never be presumptuous and over-confident of his strength, or his youth, or his luck, because the Saint might intervene at any moment and change the logical flow of things. Look at Abraham. He had accepted without a word of complaint the sacrifice of his son. So the man hit by lightening on the road . . . and . . . however . . . and yet . . . nonetheless. . . . but . . .

At that point in their discussion the rabbis have started on the sharp rise in the path. The way is covered with mud, they are slipping, getting stuck in the mud, walking with difficulty. Suddenly, what do they see? An enormous piece of rock, detached from the mountain by the rain, blocking the path.

The three rabbis fall silent, scratch their beards, smooth out their hair under their hats, mop their brows and the backs of their necks, clean their glasses, adjust their jackets, lightly wipe off dust from their pants, and then ask themselves what should they do? Return to the village to ask for help? They are worried about ridicule. Try to go around the rock? On one side of the path, there is a cliff, a mortal danger. On the other side, there is no room between the rock and the rocky wall that produced it. They would thus have to climb down the cliff, an impossibility, or climb up on the granite block, just as inconceivable, particularly for rabbis wearing caftans and moreover not accustomed to physical effort. To turn back and admit defeat? It is better to study the size, the material, the emplacement, the weight of the obstacle, the length of time of its presence there, and to come to clear and logical conclusions so as to be able, with these data in hand, to take the necessary decisions. And before all, to thank the Lord for having brought them a proof of His tangible presence and for allow-ing them to thank Him for this test which requires inventiveness, intelligence, and faith.

It's at that very moment that a peasant on the way to his field makes his appearance. He carries his hoe on the shoulder and is walking at a lively pace, that is until he encounters the rock. The sight of the rock causes him to utter a string of swear words exhibiting depth, intensity, and a meaning whose universal relevance and length make it comparable to a Shakespearean sonnet. Were these curses in Hungarian? Probably, because it is well known that, of all the languages practiced in the world, Hungarian enables you to swear in the most poetical manner. At any rate it is neither French nor English swearwords, because *merde* and "fuck"[7] lack feeling, force, expressiveness, humanity, thought, intelligence, feel for language—in short they are lacking in soul.

After having thus freed himself from the weight the surprise caused by the rock put on his heart and his stomach, the peasant becomes aware of the three rabbis' presence. Not in the least embarrassed that the three rabbis were witness to his string of swearwords that included God and all the prophets, all the saints with their virile attributes totally lacking or overgrown or overnumbered, the devil and the angels, paradise and hell, and what they were doing in there (not to mention the supposed profession, the oldest in the world it is said, of the mother of the one who put this rock on the path), the peasant politely greets the rabbis. Discussion is about to start again about the rock, a discussion destined to last and to proliferate—but our man has other things to do than get involved in a rabbinical *pilpul*, even a Talmudic one. Labor is awaiting him in the field just as, in a well-known tale, Death awaited the knight at the gates of Samarkand.

"Come rabbis, sirs, give me a hand," he says to the holy men.

And he puts down his hoe, pulls up his sleeves, and begins pushing against the rock.

The rabbis look at each other. They have no choice—they have to participate. Otherwise the whole village would know about their cowardice, their stupidity, their laziness, and their selfishness.

---

7. [In English in the French text.— TRANS.]

The four of them, shoulder to shoulder, on the peasant's loud signal of hoo! push against the rock, which starts to go down the cliff and reopens the path.

The peasant bids them good-bye with a movement of his chin and goes on his way. The rabbis look at each other silently. Then the oldest one breaks the silence: "Blah, if that one is under the illusion that you can solve problems with mere brutal force . . ."

7

Of Children

This is my youngest daughter's favorite story. Why is that? I have always tried to avoid behaving like a Yiddishe tate, and I don't for a second believe that David's character has anything in common with me. I have none of his illnesses, I am neither suicidal, nor petty. So what gives?

David makes a phone call to his daughter Rachel. This story takes place in Paris in September during the sort of fall weather that only big cities can manufacture: between the rain and the wind there's an ambient humidity that is neither warm nor cold. When you step inside somewhere you don't feel like taking your coat off. There's no sky, only buildings and rain. In the countryside, the fall sky is enormous, rapid, changing, invigorating. It makes you want all sorts of things: walks, lighting a fire in the fireplace while drinking a glass of brandy, big meals, cuddling under the feather quilt in twos, or threes, or fours. . . . In Paris this weather leads to suicide in the best cases, and in the worst, to melancholy.

The story I'm telling here thus simplifies the work of writing. No need to investigate geography, imagination, delocalization: I'm familiar with Paris. I live here. (By chance, and I wonder why I'm staying. What is it that I keep on seeking here? In a language that is not my own and that I had to learn, and I mean *had to*, when almost an adult, and a history that I'm not part of, in these stones, this landscape, that don't evoke anything for me? And yet where would I be truly at home? Where could I say that everything resembles me? Where could I identify with everything, and, more importantly, where would everything identify with me, that is, the faces, accent, memory, history, stones, landscape? Where would all—and I mean all—call to me: "You are from here, you are one of us, we accept you without reservation, without second thought?" Where I would accept boredom, satiety, and yes, even hatred—I would accept even that because it comes with human relationships.)

David lives in Paris. But he could be living elsewhere. In fact, David could be calling anywhere from anywhere.

He's calling his daughter to complain. Rachel lives in New York. She works in a museum; she is an art historian specializing in Flemish baroque. To complain is sweet. It's a way to break from solitude; to imagine that someone could help us. But someone cannot; nobody really can. But it is good, it is necessary to imagine that we are not alone.

"Listen Rachel, I'm going to kill myself. Don't interrupt me, listen to me till the end [how appropriate "till the end," that's a good one!]. I hurt everywhere; I spend all my time at the doctors and I have to take all sorts of meds, morning, noon, and night. My back is hurting, I can't lift anything. My joints ache, it's hurts to walk, and the pain is worst in my right hand so that I can't hold anything without hurting. I take pills so as to avoid going to the bathroom five times per night, I take some for high blood pressure, for cholesterol, sleeping pills in the evening, antidepressants in the morning, antianxiety pills at noon, I no longer eat cake, I have elevated triglycerides, I no longer can have sugar in my coffee, nor milk for that matter, no more Hungarian salami, no more Greek cheese, no more Bulgarian yogurt, no more Normandy butter, no more Italian pasta, no more roasted potatoes, no more Basmati rice. ... This is no life. I can't stand getting old. I no longer sleep and every night I am faced with images of my decrepitude, I see myself bedridden, impotent in my little wheelchair, and I can't stand the knowledge that I won't have enough money to afford a halfway decent retirement home. And I have to confess that the idea of having to live out my old age at my children's homes terrifies me."

Rachel tries unsuccessfully to interject: "And Mom in all this, where is she? *My* wheelchair, *my* retirement home, *my* children. ... And why are you terrified to live with your children? What have we done or not done to you?"

"Don't interrupt me, I want to tell you everything. And I'm bored, if you only knew how bored I am! I retired too early. I'm useless, no one needs me, I'm bored and I bore others from morning to night, particularly your mother. I don't see well enough to read for a whole day. I don't have enough money to see all the movies and the exhibits that I would like to see, and even less to travel . . ."

"But Dad, even if you don't want to include Mom and us, you have so many friends."

"Ha! Don't mention friends! They are mostly dead, so I can no longer visit them. But soon, ha ha. . . . I'm avoiding those that are still working because they keep talking about their work and this makes me terribly envious, and anyway, I don't give a damn about their jobs and their colleagues and their bosses and their employees. Then the worst ones are those retired like me. They are the most boring, the most insufferable. They have only four topics of conversation: money, their illnesses, their kids and grandkids, and trips. It's not possible to discuss anything with them because they think they know everything. They don't accept anyone disagreeing with them or having different views. The readers among them hit you over the head with their opinions about books . . . and at any rate, what they are seeking is not discussion, not confrontation, not learning something from you, but rather affirming their little selves that keep on shrinking and are so negligible . . . and neglected. Moreover they've read everything, so you can't tell them anything new. It's the same for movies, TV shows, politics. . . . Ah, Rachel, de Gaulle was right, old age is a shipwreck. And moreover . . ."

"But Daddy, you've always hated de Gaulle!"

"I know. But when I see the politicians we have today, those imbeciles, vain, or crooked, or all three at once—most of the time all three at once—I began to miss de Gaulle. The reasons I didn't like him were his political ideas and his behaving like a dictator. This said, he was no imbecile nor a thief, nor vain. Well, arrogant, yes, that he was. Like Mitterrand. The future that those incompetents are preparing for us, or rather for you . . . I have no desire to see it. In short, I'm fed up. I'm fed up, I'm going to eliminate myself. Paul gave me a little flask, all you need is one swallow and bye-bye, no pain, instantly."

It's too much for Rachel. She has never really analyzed her feelings for her father. . . . You probe your heart when it comes to love with a big L, the love of a guy, the one that in Hungarian is called *szerelem*, in contrast to *szeretet*, affectionate love. Love for our parents is a given, taken for granted and not analyzed; it's not a subject for reflection. But now, suddenly, for a split second she sees herself burying her father—and she realizes that it would be awfully sad, and that she loves her father very much and she would really miss him . . . of course she'd miss him. He was—good grief, why am I thinking "was," he is!—a good father along with all his weird habits and illusions and his incoherence. He raised her and her brother pretty well. And then, in her Judeo-Hungarian education, the love for one's parents is an obligation taken for granted. For granted—you must be kidding! It's repeated over and over again!

"Daddy, I beg of you. . . . You know how much we love you. You do know it."

David doesn't want and cannot hear talk of love. He stopped believing in it a long time ago. He knows or thinks he knows that it is the most misleading expression of selfishness.

Rachel continues: "How can you talk like that? You who have always taught us that feelings, ties, are the only things giving meaning to life! And all of a sudden you're saying the opposite . . ."

David interrupts her because he feels cornered. He wants to avoid any discussion of ideas where he would not come up on top.

"Daddy, don't interrupt me. It's my turn to talk," says Rachel. All that you just spewed out is false. And your political diatribe makes me laugh. I heard you rail at politicians under de Gaulle, then under Giscard, as to Mitterrand, don't even mention it! At every meal you were saying that you should have never voted for this perfidious Florentine, for this liar leading us by the tip of the nose, and his buddies and miscreants, and he is still an extreme right-winger, and he dines with Bousquet, a murderer of Jews, and he still keeps his *francisque*[8] in a drawer, and he's completely dense when it comes to Europe, and he invites Milošević to Paris, and he lies to us about his health—you had nothing but laments and despair! But you are still young, just look at

8. [The depiction of a double-headed axe used as a symbol by the Pétain government on coins, various decorations, and documents. — TRANS.]

you! Women like you. You don't even hear them. Even my girlfriends tell me you are amazingly young for your age and you are classy as can be. Yes, yes! And then we all need you. Firstly Mom, then also Freddy and I. You cannot, you don't have the right to do this to us!"

"You see," says David, "you are proving me right, and your girl-friends likewise. 'Young for your age,' that means: you're really old but you don't look it. But age is there. I'll never forget my father who when eighty flexed his muscles to show me how he was still in good shape. When I congratulated him, he told me 'I don't look like eighty'—and he paused for a moment after which he stated 'but I do know it!' Listen Rachel, I have reached a decision. Your arguments—and they are not arguments, you are only saying all this to make me happy, even though what you're telling me doesn't make me happy at all—in short your arguments aren't going to keep me in this world. It's not true that you need me. No one needs me. You're getting along pretty well without me. You and Freddy no longer even live here, we almost never see you, and you'll do fine as well after my death."

Rachel all of a sudden feels that despair is lurking underneath her father's speech. Or it might be weariness, fatigue. Perhaps she should take him seriously. She tells herself that she would be sorry for the rest of her life if she didn't try to do something.

"All right, Daddy. Don't do anything. I'm taking the first available plane and I'll be there before you know it. Wait for me, I beg of you. We need to talk. You know that we love you so very much. Very much. I repeat, we love you and need you. Even if we don't see you every day. The fact that you are there gives me courage. It reassures me. I know that I can call you, send you an e-mail, and that you would give me some advice. If you no longer want to live for yourself, at least do it for us. It's your duty. Daddy, please please wait for me. We'll talk, discuss things, and talk some more, as long as needed. I will convince you to stay with us. You'll wait for me, you promise? You swear? I'll be in Paris tomorrow. In the meanwhile take a tranquilizer, go have a beer with your buddy Jacques, or go watch a musical comedy—and then I'll be home. You promise, OK?"

"OK," says David. "Do you want me to pick you up at the airport? Send me your schedule by e-mail."

Next, David calls his son, who is an optician in London.

"Listen kiddo, I've decided to kill myself. That's all."

The poor guy, who is in the process of helping a customer, almost falls down. He has to sit down. He must keep his countenance. "Daddy, I'll call you back right away."

David doesn't want any argument. "It's not worth it. Don't call me back. That's all I had to say. Any discussion would be useless. Hugs and kisses, ciao."

And he hangs up.

As soon as the customer is out the door, Freddy, shaken up, wonders if he should first call his sister in New York, or call his father back to get some explanations. He is of course familiar with his father's propensity for big tragic and theatrical scenes. All the family is used to them. And yet . . . suicide is new. Usually it is "I'm going away you'll never see me again I'm fed up with this family for which I work like an idiot like a mule and what is it I'm getting in return . . ." David prefers the presence of a large audience, that of the whole family, for his dramatic acts. This time he has to content himself with just one ear—but Freddy assumes that the rest of the family has already been informed. He decides on a direct confrontation. He dials his father's Parisian phone number.

David serves him the same dish as he did his daughter, with a few variants such as "I no longer get along at all with your mother; we are at war all the time" (he couldn't come up with this one with Rachel because she would have taken her mother's side), and "I'm no longer interested in women, and at any rate, in the state I'm in, I'm good for nothing "(that one was a bit too much, he thinks afterward, after all I'm talking to my son, not to one of my buddies).

"Daddy, don't do anything foolish," says the son. "Everything you're telling me is nonsense. One doesn't kill oneself because of arguing with one's wife. You just have a touch of the blues. Let it pass. Every year you get depressed on the eve of Rosh Hashanah. You can't stand the thought that a year has passed, and that ten days later, you have to fast for a whole day. On December 31, you're going to do it again . . ."

"OK, OK," answers David. "Let's not talk about it anymore. I'm hanging up. You won't see me again. Have a happy life."

"Hey, Dad, that's crazy. What's going on? Wait. I'm taking the next train and I'll be there. We need to talk. It seems to be important. I've lots of things to tell you. Things that I've never talked about. I'll be home before the evening. Don't do anything crazy. In the meanwhile, take a tranquilizer, and I'll be there before you'll know it. Promise? Say you promise? We'll have dinner together and then we can have a conversation. A serious one. We'll see each other in a little while, OK? We could even go out somewhere, if you want, and if you want us to talk just the two of us. And I'll stay several days if you want. Hugs and kisses, one thousand times. I'm closing the store and I'm rushing to the train station. Tell Mom!"

And Freddy hangs up.

David, smiling broadly, goes to the kitchen and tells his wife: "Zelda, the kids are coming to Paris for the holidays. Both of them. And they're even paying for their own trips!"

8

Wailing

This story is a gift a friend gave me in the street. I was happily bicycling one morning on my way to work when another rider, non-Jewish, the painter Ivan Messac, addressed me: "Hey, Adam, I've got a joke for you!"
* And here it is.*

Two Jews are praying in front of the Wailing Wall in Jerusalem (at this point I have to ask myself, do I need to say it was in Jerusalem? As if everyone didn't know it. Perhaps even the Iranian government knows it. And it might even know how old the Wall is, and its origin—and there lies the problem, the problem of that government and the ones following it—or those accepting it. They can't forgive us our existence. And what's the use of saying "Two Jews are praying in front of the Wall"? Who else would pray there? Two Iranian ministers of state? One should be writing like Hemingway, concise, brief, straight to the point, like Flaubert, screaming while rereading himself.)

   When I went to Israel for the first time, the Wall still belonged to Jordan, and I wasn't able to see it. It was in 1962, before the Six Day War. (How it seems distant now! Peace, a solution, was still possible then. My kibbutz was a left-leaning one. It had a portrait of Marx in the dining hall along with one of Ferhat Abbas, one of the leaders of the Algerian independence movement. And twenty years later, it was still possible—at least that's what I thought, I believed that with time.... Of course, time... Until the day when Alberto Moravia shocked me by telling me that time won't help. "Look at the war in Ireland... five hundred years and it's not over yet. The Israeli/Palestinian conflict, compared to Ireland, is only at its beginnings. Unless..." Today, in despair,

I'm asking Moravia's spirit and myself: unless what? In those days Israeli politicians, Ben-Gurion, Golda Meir, had at least a vision. I'm not saying that it was a good one, but at least they were people with integrity, with ideas ... while today, over there as here, petty politicians are thinking of themselves as the only goal, and money as the only idea ...)

In 1962 we could see only a bit of the old city from the spire of the Dormition church. From up there, Israeli soldiers posted behind sandbags were hurling insults at the Jordanian soldiers and vice versa. The Jordanians were positioned on the other side of a fortified wall that divided Jerusalem in two, just before the church. When I returned thirty-four years later, I, a die-hard atheist,[9] "prayed"—well, let's say meditated. I was very moved in front of this wall. I felt I was facing the very symbol of my origins, of their materialization—even while remembering the calculation of a mathematician friend. He demonstrated to me the very small probability that he and I, two Ashkenazi Jews, had ancestors whose flocks were grazing two thousand years ago on the lands of the kingdom of Judea. He imagined rather our ancestors on the shores of the Volga: Slavs, Judaicized Khazars ...

So, what difference does it make? None to me, and even less to anti-Semites.

Oh, well. Here I'm chatting while our two friends are praying. And they are truly praying rather than sacrificing to God knows what symbol of an intellectual yearning for belonging.

One, Mister Eisenschmutz, gaunt, small, elegant, his head covered with a *kepele* in embroidered silk, prays with fervor and a French accent (this is a rhetorical zeugma of the sort "I'm Hungarian and robbed"). Mister Eisenschmutz is French. (Even though the companies he owns are based in the Cayman Islands, the Virgin Islands, and Antigua, Mister Eisenschmutz is neither Cayman, nor Virgin, nor Antiguan. No, he's French. His motive for setting up the headquarters of his businesses in these barely existing improbable distant islands are humanitarian. He wanted to give work to the unemployed Caymans and Virgins. Mister Eisenschmutz is in the field of debt collections. And it is well known that it is in the Virgin Islands that one collects—debts

---

9. Montherlant writes that the only thing stupider than the proofs of God's existence are the proofs of his nonexistence.

that is—the best). He rocks back and forth as is proper. After the usual prayers, as if ashamed of himself, he whispers his personal wish, the one for which he has come here, perhaps even directly from Antigua.

"Lord let me have one million dollars. I really need it. I've the possibility of realizing a fabulous deal. It happens that just at this moment I don't have enough available liquid, otherwise I wouldn't dare bother You. However, if you could immediately free one million dollars I could buy a whole building in the old Jewish neighborhood of Budapest. The owner just died two days ago and his only daughter, sick and not very smart, has urgent need of money to bury her father, to pay the inheritance tax, to get healthcare for herself, to put her disabled mother in a nursing home, and whatever else—I don't know what those Hungarian Jews do with their money. I heard that this daughter is in a bind and would agree to one million. The building is old and in need of repair, but even this way it is worth at least five times as much. It's an art nouveau building with at least two hundred apartments with several inner courtyards opening on each other. You know this type of housing from the Austro-Hungarian empire. . . . When new, this building must have been magnificent. I would register it on the list of historical monuments, then I would apply to the city for a grant to restore it. I have friends at city hall in Budapest. So I could get a part of my million back right away—excuse me, I mean Your million. Then I'll discover that the building is in too bad a shape to restore it. So I'll have it demolished and in its stead I'll put up a big ultramodern building, the kind Hungarians have never seen. I'll sell it one very expensive apartment at a time to foreigners, I mean other than Hungarians, such as Arab princes, African kings, or American Jews. You follow me, Lord? Please have pity on Your son. I deserve it. You know how much I donated to Israel. And I'll give it more. And even more if You help me in this deal. You know the number of charity organizations I contribute to. In one of the synagogues of Petah-Tikvah, there is even a Eisenschmutz study room. So help me Lord to make this superb deal. It is unique; never again will I have such an opportunity."

Having finished his prayer (we should call it his lament—after all isn't the purpose of this wall to be a place of lamentations over the destruction of the Temple?) Mister Eisenschmutz slips his small piece of paper with his small request into a gap between two enormous thousand-year-old stones of the Kotel.

Right next to the Caymano-Virgin Frenchman, very near him, stands Mister Achocron, a bearded man dressed all in black. He is praying with a Moroccan accent, every word loud enough for all to hear.

He asks his God to come to his aid, to give him one hundred dollars so he can get through the month. My business, yet again went bankrupt, and I am penniless. I know what You are thinking. I am perfectly aware of it, and yet You are wrong—forgive me for saying this to You. You are mistaken about me. You are saying that this dishonest Achocron would do better to look for a real and honest job instead of setting up businesses which, always, because of his clumsy relation with money, go bankrupt. I promise You, Lord, never again! If You help me, I'll give up the profession of dishonest entrepreneur. You see, I'm going along with Your thinking: I did say "dishonest." I'll look for wage work and I'll go into psychoanalysis to get cured of my problem with money. I swear! Help me for the last time, I beg of You! My wife left me two days ago and she is demanding that I reimburse her the money she invested in my business, not to mention the child support she is claiming in order to raise our two children alone. I don't have a shekel to buy food. My sister-in-law, You know, the one who's in business, owes me money at the end of the month. In the meanwhile, I don't know what I'm going to live on. I'll look for work, I'll sell things, my collections of paintings and photographs, my butterflies, my matchstick boxes, I'll think of something, You know, You know me, I've always gotten by, but now, just for the next few days, it's too hard. . . . Help me Lord! One hundred dollars would be enough.

And like thousands and thousands of other Jews before him since the destruction of the Temple, Mister Achocron too inserts his piece of paper carefully folded in four into an interstice of the Wall, before starting another prayer.

At this very moment, Mister Eisenschmutz, having heard everything and carefully listened to it all, suddenly turns toward Mister Achocron and, pulling a hundred-dollar bill from his pocket says to him:

"Listen buddy. Here's a hundred bucks—and now get lost and leave the two of us alone!"

9

Of Education

This story is well known. A philosopher friend of mine even cited it in his book about (against) God. It has had a life of its own. And beware: if one day, as is probable, France were to have an Islamic government, this story would even be told on the National Assembly benches! It is indeed emblematic. No story can better sum up the contradictions besetting us. (Us who?)

The Lévys are a couple of French intellectuals, as they exist in the thousands, as I know dozens. They are free thinkers, they say; the literate would call them agnostics, and they would be called atheists in common parlance. They exhibit a touch of anarchism. Neither God nor master, they're wont to say, particularly no God, given the present state of knowledge, of science. . . . How ridiculous! And to speak of God after Auschwitz . . . excuse me . . . Once a year, as if accidentally at the last minute, they remember the customs of their grandparents, whom they have known, and even that of their parents, and they rush to the nearest synagogue. There the *shames*, who had never seen them before, doesn't know them. They try to hide their embarrassment by making a bit of a joke, so they tell him: "We are Yom Kippur Yids." And the *shames* replies: "No, you are Kol Nidre Yids."[10]

Mr. and Mrs. Lévy thus decide to enroll their little Maurice in a private high school run by Salesian priests.

(One more parenthesis: from whence came little Maurice's name? Hungarians know this quite well. Good heavens, but of course it's Móricka, the child hero of all Hungarian stories, whether they be Jew-

10. Kol Nidre is the first prayer on the evening of Yom Kippur.

ish or not! "Ahogy azt a Móricka elképzeli!" This is just as little Maurice imagines it—thus totally unimaginable, impossible, invented. And who was this Móricka? The ancestor of little Maurice, or rather the first historical Móricka, was the very young son of the rabbi of Tiszaeszlár, a Hungarian village of the great plain. In the last years of the nineteenth century he caused his father and the notables of the Jewish community to be brought in front of the courts by accusing them of ritual murders. He claimed he saw them cut the neck of a young Christian girl of the village so as to mix her blood with the matzo bread of Passover. The Jews were acquitted thanks to a lawyer member of the Hungarian nobility, and Móricka had to emigrate/flee to the United States. End of the parenthesis? But do you really believe it ended? Has it ever ended and was it really only a parenthesis? You'd have to be naive, or ignorant of history, or blind and deaf, or too afraid to face reality, or perhaps too lazy, to believe that.)

So let's get back to France, where no such thing could ever happen, except for the Dreyfus Affair (contemporary to the Tiszaeszlár Affair), the Vél d'Hiv, Maurice Papon (a Fifth Republic minister and the police prefect of Paris), the friendship of Mitterrand and Bousquet, the Fofana/Ilan Halimi Affair, the anti-Semitic comments of the prime minister Raymond Barre . . . is that all?[11] Well almost, at least for the time being.

"Enough of lay, republican, and compulsory schools," exclaimed the Lévys, even though they are both the product of these schools, with the results we are familiar with, that is, excellence. But times

---

11. In July 1942, the Parisian police detained thirteen thousand Jews in the winter cycle stadium (the Vélodrome d'Hiver, which went down in history by its abbreviation, Vél d'Hiv) before sending them to extermination camps after a brief stopover in France. Maurice Papon (who died a comfy death in his bed in 2007) was general secretary of the police prefecture of the Gironde Département (province) during the Occupation and was responsible for the deportation of a great number of Jews, among whom were many children. And to show he hadn't lost the knack, he also ordered the killing of peaceful Algerian protesters in Paris in 1961. Bousquet was in charge of Jewish affairs in the Vichy collaborationist government. He was also a friend of François Mitterrand, the "Socialist" president who routinely invited him for dinner at the Elysée mansion in the nineteen eighties. Ilan Halimi was a young Jew tortured to death in a Paris suburb in 2006 by a street gang led by a Senegalese-French by the name of Fofana.

have changed. Children no longer learn anything. The methods are stupid, the national directives idiotic, the other students are illiterate and drag little Maurice and his grades down to their level. Yet knowledge is the only thing we can really own. Oh, there's school, education, end-of-the-year report card, years of preparation to be accepted in one of the French "grandes écoles," the exams, the exam results, the ranking of the results. Maurice, you'll finally go to a real school, that of the Salesian Fathers—they're the best. You'll learn Latin like your father, Greek like your grandfather, advanced math, chemistry, and physics like your other grandfather (and the mother, where is she in all this? And the mother's mother, are they irrelevant?), a bit of sport, not too much because it's for the children of the suburbs[12] (though it's true, they are on the left there, but . . .). In short, you'll come out of there with a real education. You'll be ready for whatever life has to offer, like Captain Dreyfus, the Rabbi of Tiszaeszlár, the detainees of the Vél d'Hiv and Ilan Halimi.

At the end of the first day of class, the Lévy parents impatiently wait for little Maurice. They have both come home early from work and would have liked to pick up Maurice at school, something their son had strictly forbidden. "Please! Don't embarrass me! This is not kindergarten!"

The Lévys wait for their only son in the living room. And here is our big little one! And kisses and hugs, and how was it?

"It was great," says the little one who's already big. The other kids are cool. We had fun. During recess we played—"

"OK, OK," Mister Lévy interrupts. "Recess is nice, but in class, the courses, how were they?"

"That was also good, we learned all sorts of things . . ."

Mister Lévy is on pins and needles. Madame Lévy silently keeps her misty eyes on her beloved offspring. (Does this reminds you of your own past?) "Oh, he's so smart!"

The father can't stand it. He keeps asking what did they learn in class? What courses did he have? How are the teachers? Are they all clergy or are they also lay teachers?

12. [The suburbs in France are the equivalent of the inner city in the United States. — TRANS.]

Little Maurice answers patiently-impatiently. Parents can be such a bore. School is all right while you're there, but it's no fun to keep playing school at home.

The father wants to know all the details. What have they learned, was Maurice called on in class, was he able to answer . . .

"We had math, geography, and religion," says an exhausted Maurice.

Mister Lévy had forgotten this small detail. They were going to be taught religion. He'll have to drop by the school, fix this problem. It's obviously very awkward. But they should have thought about this, the teachers. Well, and us too, he admits.

"So what did you do in your religion class? (Oh, this really really hurts. I'll go see the principal as soon as I have a moment . . .)

"Lots of stuff."

"Exactly what?"

"Oh I don't know. For instance we spoke about Jesus Christ. And then I also learned something I didn't know. There are three gods: the father, the son, and the holy ghost—"

Mister Lévy jumps up. "No and no! Absolutely not! Listen to me, Maurice, and listen well to what I'm telling you—it's very important. There is only one God." A silence. "And we don't believe in Him."

10

Of Numbers

It used to be that Jews prayed, they studied, they worked. The story that follows might thus seem atypical. And yet . . .

Schönberger Izráel was one of my ancestors (the grandfather of my paternal grandmother) and he lived in Hungary in the village of . . . let's say Királyhelmec. The village name is just for show (literary pretensions!). In fact he lived in Nagyvárad, but Nagyvárad was a town—it was cultured and moreover developed—and my story would lose some of its credibility (but who is asking a Jewish *witz* to be credible?). I'll thus locate my story in Királyhelmec, because it was a village. In reality it was the birthplace of my grandfather Bíró Márk. And also for the ease of pronunciation. And also I've written a lot already about Nagyvárad—perhaps too much.

I'm not in the least bit familiar with Királyhelmec. I've never gone there. I don't even know where it is. However, I am familiar with the villages of the great Hungarian plain and I have a very clear idea of this burg. I can perfectly visualize the church, city hall, the best houses near the church, right on the square with the war memorial, and the war monument itself, as in France: lots of names from World War I, a bit fewer from World War II (but still more than in France). . . . Countries resemble each other by their stupidity, their misfortunes, their unjustified hatreds that are so strong, so inexplicable, and a thousand times explained and justified by every politician. These monuments to the dead, everywhere in Europe, these futile dead . . . and yet we must honor the dead, otherwise what meaning could our lives have? Then there are the other houses on the main street, with their long verandas perpendicular to the street and vegetable gardens behind the houses, then modest dwellings almost at the end of the village, and at the end, the miserable shelters of the Tziganes, almost outside the village, where there is no longer any street, no running water, no electricity, no longer anything except for dust, mud, shame, hatred and more hatred. . . . And I don't know where the Jews were living—at any rate, how can this be important? They are no longer living anywhere, neither them nor their descendants. The Jews of the Hungarian countryside have all been taken to the camps, with no exception.

Schönberger Izráel was a pipe maker—it's true. He had many children—that's just as true. I already talked about him in another book where I had him experience strange adventures, less true. He had a neighbor, a certain Loewinger Leopold. (In Hungarian the family name precedes the given name. You must have noticed this from the very beginning of the book. This is a test.) While Izráel was intelligent and hardworking, he had only a secondhand knowledge of the outside world. He had never traveled; he hated any travel, as it made him feel unstable, insecure. He had never gone farther than the neighboring burg, barely a town. Thus he only knew of Hungary's capital, Budapest, through the gossip of the few acquaintances and neighbors who had gone there, or rather who had to go there. They went there only by necessity, because it was far away, and when there, Jewish villagers were terrified of the city that was Budapest in the twenties. So why would Izráel travel? He had a family, he was working, praying, studying—he thus obeyed the commandments. What else could a pious Jew do? In truth some might find this matter for discussion. The end result of study is knowledge, and knowledge requires openness: to others, to the world. However, that is a modern conception of study. Knowledge must be of God. For Izráel, to study meant to read the Bible, that's all. But since he was curious, he read and listened a lot.

His neighbor Loewinger Leopold was also curious about everything, but in contrast to Izráel, he couldn't stay in one place. He was not very pious, and even barely that. He only went to the synagogue because he was afraid of what people would say if he didn't. One day he decided to go visit the capital. No other reason than the desire for knowledge, he said. The village was surprised. What is he going to do

in this Gehanna, this Sodom, this Gomorrah, this vice-filled Baby-
lon, in the Leviathan gorge itself, in this impenetrable forest, in the
sound and fury? The villagers warned him and envied him. It's easy
for Leopold to travel! He had no wife thus no children, no ties, he can
go wherever he fancies. He can close his shop temporarily, which he
does often to go buy merchandise.

In reality, Leopold had a secret reason to go to Budapest: he wanted
to find a wife. Of course, the local matchmaker had offered him several
prospects. Leopold was a good match, except that he wanted a lady, a
woman of culture and manners. Ladies, there were none in Királyhelmec. Honest women, yes (a bit too honest for Leopold's taste), good
housewives, even pretty, there were, but ladies, no! Leopold didn't
know any ladies of the sort he imagined. Yes, he wanted to bring back
a wife from the capital. One like they had never seen in Királyhelmec,
with dresses custom-made by big city seamstresses and petticoats,
oh!—and lingerie, way too exciting to imagine!

Izráel stopped him in the street one day. "Leopold, take a good
look around you, open your eyes, and tell us everything in detail when
you come back."

Leopold's opinion was more important to Izráel than the verbal
accounts of merchants who went regularly to Budapest. So upon his
return Leopold would be able to depict the city in a way that would
satisfy Izráel.

So it was done.

Leopold came back one month later. One month is not very long for
a journey. (Remember that Montaigne's trip from Bordeaux to Rome
lasted several months.) It took a whole day to get there and a whole day
to come back. And once there, the traveler had to find his bearings,
smell the air, then inquire from each passerby resembling a fellow Jew
where to find the recipient of letters of recommendation. And then
to discuss, palaver, exchange views, explore the smallest details at
length, inquire about families with marriageable women, visit these
families, and then meet with a matchmaker. And hope that fate would
smile upon him.

And now Leopold is back in Királyhelmec.

He has barely gotten into his house, barely shaken the dust of the road from his coat and his mind, barely has he slipped back into the skin of the village shopkeeper of Királyhelmec, which has always been his except the last month when he was a city dweller looking for a spouse, and Izráel is already knocking at his door. The stories Leopold is about to serve him bring with them all the positive aspects of travel but none of its inconveniences. The anticipation of the tales he is about to hear has already filled him with pleasure.

"So, Leopold, tell me. First, what did you do all this time?"

Leopold has seen, heard, and listened. He couldn't, wouldn't, admit the true purpose of his trip—which, while it was not a failure, while it was filled with promises and future, was neither conclusive nor concluded for the time being. As I've said, in addition to visits paid to families with marriageable daughters, he also met with a *shadchen*, a matchmaker, who introduced several other young girls to him. And now he had to send letters and return to the capital with gifts . . . in short, all the effort, all the preparations for the sixty years of happiness to come, to hope, and wait for.

"Tell me what you've seen."

And Leopold dives into his narrative.

He has seen a Jew who, without being really pious and without ever attending the synagogue, didn't work on the Sabbat and was eating kosher. He made the acquaintance of one who was a Marxist, a revolutionary, and hoped for a world without exploitation. He met one who was the head of an enormous enterprise employing thousands of workers and employees and was earning in the millions. He dined with a Jew who, after reading the writing of a Viennese scholar by the name of Freud, had become adept at psychoanalysis, the science invented by this Freud. He spoke with a fellow Jew who was Zionist and dreamed of one day settling in Palestine. He listened to an amateur musician who played the violin masterfully. Leopold attended a reading by an avant-garde poet. He endured explanations by a Jew enthralled by mathematics. He had conversations with one who had studied law, he walked with a Jew who spoke seven languages, he had a discussion with a Jew who had visited the United States, he had . . .

Schönberger Izráel interrupts him; he's impressed, amazed, flabbergasted. "I see that you haven't wasted your time!" He exclaimed.

"All those people! Amazing how many people you met . . . and they were so diverse. What a multitude of persons, what diversity among Jews in a big city!"

"Not at all," replies Leopold very calm. "It was always the same Jew."

11

Thirsty for More

My mother's sister, who, toward the end of her life, was fond of distant travels,
was a whimsical and odd person. I'll call her Sarah here. If you want to know her
real name and story, you can read it in my familial autobiography, One Must
Also Be Hungarian *(self publicity, self glorification—the only sincere ones).*
    And don't tell me that the following story isn't Jewish!

This time Sarah, who lived in Switzerland, was doing Tunisia. She had
already done Egypt, Malaysia, and Singapore. She had offered herself
Iceland, India, and Italy in alphabetical order as well as all the other
countries whose names began with I. She did this in guided group
tours. She found being a sheep in a flock reassuring. It made it possible for her to avoid confrontation with local sheep (all mangy) as the
conscientious tour operators in their globalized wisdom had planned
on visiting only the aseptic and presentable corners of the pastures.
Moreover, traveling in a group spared Sarah from the need to prepare
for the trip herself with fastidious and complicated readings, readings that had been previously digested in her stead by ventriloquist
guides. The Organization also spared her any concern about organization prior to and during the stay—and a Helvetically organized trip
was less expensive than a disorganized one. And how could she have
been invited to the captain's table during her latest cruise if she hadn't
been part of a group? And how would she have been able to meet, for
instance, during her trip to Mexico, these fascinating Swiss group
members if she had been traveling by herself? No, she wouldn't have
met anyone besides a few uninteresting Mexicans.
    The trip to Tunisia included crossing the desert by bus. So they had

been told to pack this, bring along that, wear this, make plans for the rest, not do too . . . , good, enough, sufficiently, not at all, particularly not, and even if. . . . You know all those preparations for travel in the desert, you, who in contrast to me . . .

So there, you can see them climb into the bus. A gleaming German contraption, brightly colored pretty symbols of the *Wirtschaftswunder*, the economic miracle. It has been washed, shampooed, and coiffed. On its side is written in huge golden letters: *Sicher reisen: Trückmüsch-Reisen!* (Safe Travel with *Trückmüsch* Tours!)—this in order to advertise their services all along the journey, particularly in the desert. The travelers settle down, and they too are washed, shampooed, curled, coiffed with all the hair cutely blown up by the wind announcing the Sacred Thrill of the Great Adventure.

Look at them riding in the desert. The sun is cooking the body of the bus. From time to time, they speed by an oasis and they get a glimpse of its two miraculously surviving cadaverous palm trees and some adorable kids in rags, picturesquely dirty just like on TV, running—that is those able to run—a few meters behind the bus. Even though the air conditioning in the bus is set at maximum, it isn't really cooling and it's getting increasingly hot.

Sarah feels she's about to faint. What a stupid idea to come to this country. She had been warned: don't go to an Arab country. They are all thieves and anti-Semites. She should have listened . She had gulped down both her bottles of mineral water a long time ago, and now she moans. "*Mein Gott*, I'm so thirsty! Lord, I'm going to die of thirst. Oh, I'm so, so thirsty!"

Her fellow travelers aren't listening to her. Their mouths too are dry and the heat has wiped them out. Let Sarah complain—who cares! They all have their burdens to carry, they're all thirsty.

But Sarah keeps on complaining. "Thirsty! I'm thirsty! Oh how am I thirsty! Oh, oh, I can't stand it anymore! I want to drink! *Oy vey*, how awful, oh I'm so thirsty! Have pity on me!"

Her neighbor in misfortune, a fortunate German, born with a ruddy complexion made even ruddier by the present circumstances, is sticking to Sarah, not because of lust, as this is surely not the time to make a pass at her, but because of the bumps of the bus and sweat.

He can't stand hearing her moan another minute. Moved by a proto-Christian feeling and even more by exasperation, he hands her his own bottle of water, hot like the air, hot like everything in this bus, in this desert, in this country, in this continent.

Sarah, without uttering any thanks, throws herself on the plastic bottle and drinks avidly. She lets go with an obnoxious and noisy burp before returning the almost empty bottle to its owner.

She is quiet. The bus is rolling on. There is a complete silence. One can only hear the engine and the hum of the air conditioner.

Then suddenly, a small voice can be heard at the back of the bus. I recognize Sarah.

"*Oy vey tsoress,*[13] how terrible—I was so thirsty!"

13. [*Tsoress* means "troubles," "calamities." — TRANS.]

12

Of Privileges

This story calls upon history itself. It must serve for the political edification of the younger generations and reinforce their class consciousness in the spirit of Marxist-Leninist teachings.

Late in the evening a rumor spreads around Warsaw: tomorrow there will be meat in the big butcher shop on the Isaac Bashevis Singer Square. (I hope you're not so naive as to swallow the tale that in Poland in the sixties they named a square after a Polish Jewish author writing in Yiddish and living in the United States!)

The rumor ambles and rambles. It would be interesting to follow the path of a rumor in the process of spreading. From one neighbor to another, as if perchance with a peek into the house next door when borrowing a couple of eggs, in the inns, the bars when drinkers are still capable of exchanging information, during endless travels in crowded buses as people go to work and are conversing with each other to occupy themselves, to occupy other things than their legs, even if only the mouth, in bed between lovers when the flesh has been satiated and when they don't know what to talk about and they are taking a discreet peek at their watches on the floor next to the bed and thinking of the Other (the legitimate one) waiting at home, and they should hurry there to seek shelter and for order to reign. (We are in Warsaw after all!)[14] Rumor of a meat delivery doesn't, however, reach the members of the Council of Ministers nor those of the Central Com-

14. This historical allusion is an old person's joke. I won't explain it to you. Too much knowledge can harm, too little can kill. Just go look it up in the dictionary or in the history book of your high school years, or better yet, Google it.

mittee (of the Party, what else?), because these people don't go to the cafés, don't take the bus, never borrow eggs. They have their private/ reserved shops where one can find everything, meat, fish, lovers, mistresses, and the rest, the necessary and the superfluous, and because in these Kouncils and Kommittees, there are only men (except for the sole Komrade Woman, always there for photo ops and stats) and these men don't give a hoot about cooking.

And in the former Kommunist countries, former East, former Central (we are speaking of Europe here), rumors like jokes travel (or rather traveled!) faster than elsewhere.

At any rate, the next day at dawn, a very large crowd is squeezed in front of the famous butcher shop in the unnamable square. Because they said there would be meat. Because it was years since Poles had seen any meat. Because, according to rumors, Polish meat was sent to Russia. (In Hungary, in Romania they were saying the same thing. Perhaps it was true . . .) Because the Poles hated the Russians. Since forever, since the Russians with the help of the Prussians and the Austrians had split Poland up and shared the pieces to the point where there was No More Country, No More Poland—simply no more. And perhaps they'd already hated them before that; I don't know enough about the Polish soul and Polish history. Hate doesn't need meat, it can live on very little!

Thus there's a crowd, a line. Well, let's say a "line" in the Eastern mode. It seldom resembles the queue of city gentlemen at the Bond Street bus stop. It's anything but a queue; it's a conglomerate of moving, tangled-up bodies. It's I am stronger than you so get out of the way, I'm violent, step on it or I'm going to step on your foot, I'm aggressive, I'll punch your chest with my elbow and I'll take your place, I'm secretary of the Party, I knee you in the thigh and get in front of you, I am the butcher's brother-in-law so I can go in before anyone else to greet him. . . . And also though more rarely: I'm older than you, so let me pass, I'm pregnant, give me your place, I'm blind, get out of the way. At the end of the line there is left a scrawny young man, a nonviolent, bottom-rung member of the Party, neither single mother, nor nun doing penance, nor unfrocked priest, nor holder of a work medal, nor veteran, nor Resistance hero, nor cousin of the butcher, nor student of the nation; but with eyes, ears, and legs fit for walking.

The store doesn't open until eight o'clock—and it is only five-thirty in the morning in the Warsaw February. Thus, minus eighteen degrees Celsius, dirty frozen snow, moonless starless night without hope. You can see, you can feel all this from where you are, at home, nice and cozy under the comforter, from where you are listening to me if you're not sleeping.

The crowd is dense; they are close to a thousand—and more and more people are streaming in. It's a flood. "Mouth to ear" communication is much more efficient than the radio, the newspapers, and the TV, to the point that one wonders what's their use? The people squash and insult each other, patiently push and push again, each holding a net shopping bag. Some of them even forget what they are waiting for and why. The women are covered with enormous headscarves wrapped three times around themselves; the men's heads disappear under their scarves and caps. An acrid smell of bad alcohol and cheap tobacco makes for a more friendly atmosphere. Unlabeled vodka bottles are passed around. Even while shoving each other, they tap their feet, dance in place, tell political stories, and also, but more rarely, because there's no danger and thus it's less exciting, dirty jokes.

Time drags, falls asleep. It is only six o'clock . . . Then suddenly it's awakened by the shock of a commanding voice tearing up the night in front of the still closed door of the shop: "There won't be enough meat for everyone!"

A threatening silence ensues.

"Go home Jews! Out! Let them leave, we'll have nothing for them!"

Calmly, without uttering a word, for they are used to it, almost ashamed, head down, the Jews come out of the crowd.

The others, reassured, remain. This is as it has happened since forever, so there's no need for an epilogue. We know that. We know the others, our relations with the others. And this will never change. Them and us. Neither them nor us.

The crowd waits, the sky barely lightens up. A timid and dirty gray, low and suffocating, that's their sky. Cold reigns. How do you expect . . . ?

It is seven o'clock. What else can they do but wait? How about squeezing closer to the woman next to you, secretly fondling her, slipping a furtive and sometimes tolerated hand in between the many layers of clothes. . . . The beginning (or the end) of an adventure. Or drinking, some are already drunk.

Then the same voice, again:

"Good people! We just learned that the meat shipment is smaller than expected. There will be meat today—as an exception and contrary to other days, and please forgive us—only for Party members. I hope that our friends, citizens who are not Party members, will understand our predicament. Tomorrow as usual everyone will be able to find in this shop the piece of meat they need and their favorite cuts."

Rumblings, yells, fists raised and immediately lowered, because at that very instant, a police bus shows up on the square. Policemen in uniform, nightsticks attached to their belts, slowly step out.

The crowd becomes sparser, some people quickly return to bed, some lucky men go home with lucky women, and vice versa, or to the already opened bars, or go directly to the factory at the other side of town.

The Party members, still numerous and in all ways identical to the nonmembers, keep on pressing, trampling, fighting, caressing each other; they keep on trying to open up a selfish path to the butcher shop. At least they can be assured they'll be able to buy some meat. What a feast! It's been so long. . .

It's past eight o'clock, and the store blinds remain mutely down.

It's then that the man, finally visible wearing a shiny leather coat, addresses the people a third time. To the members of the Party: "Comrades! For strategical reasons and in order to not give an opening to the enemies of the working class who are always ready to denigrate the progress of socialism, our leaders have decided to postpone the selling of meat this morning. See you tomorrow, then. And let's close ranks for the victory that will soon be ours!"

The police in tight ranks slowly advance toward the shop. The people look to the ground and, dragging their feet, slowly disperse in a frightening and anxiety-ridden silence. Suddenly there is a grumbling:

"Jew bastards! They're always the ones getting preferential treatment!"

13

Environment

This anecdote was given to me in Hungary, in Leányfalu, on the shore of the Danube, in my favorite restaurant, Határcsárda (the inn at the border), by my friend Balázs Péter during a summer lunch in the company of another friend, Demény András, who had been in the same class—in grade school! And we are sixty-five years old!

We engaged in an interesting and fruitful discussion about the story: was it, as I thought, a typical political story (although under camouflage) of the Communist years in Eastern Europe, or on the contrary, a story that was very Jewish, very revelatory of the Talmudic mind as my two friends were claiming?

Let the listener be the judge.

A Talmudic student, a yeshiva *bocher*, has to go on a trip. He wants to visit his parents for the holidays and does not wish to be saddled with valuable objects, in order to start the new year pure, free from the weight of earthly possessions. Being mistrustful of his landlady, he doesn't dare leave his meager possessions, his scant treasures, in his room closet. So he goes to see his rabbi, his teacher, the only person he trusts in the town.

"*Rebbe*, I'm going home to be with my family for the holidays. You know that I own practically nothing, but this nothing is of value to me, even though it's more sentimental than monetary. You're the only person I can entrust with my things during my absence. I don't want to leave them in my room because I risk not finding them again upon my return, and I would have no way of proving that I had left them there. Without a witness. . . And I really couldn't ask my landlady to sign a receipt! That would be an insulting mark of mistrust, and it would ruin our relationship. I wish to avoid conflict. I wish to avoid any concern that would distract me from my studies. I wish to be able to study in peace. I thus would like to leave my things with you."

The rabbi sees no inconvenience in this; on the contrary he feels honored by this show of trust.

The student empties the contents of his canvas bag on the table: a few bills, some change, a silver candleholder, a ring with a stone, and a pocket watch.

The rabbi looks carefully at everything, then he stands up to call the *shames* from the next room.

"Look," he tells him. "You're witness to what our young friend is leaving in my hands during his absence. Please, count the money. Good. There is also a candleholder, a ring, and a watch. We agree then, you've seen everything? You'll testify, if need be, that the student present here has entrusted me with these objects."

It is uselessly solemn and a bit formal, but the rabbi wants to show his student that he is taking him seriously, him and his request.

The *shames* approves and confirms everything.

"I thank you," says the rabbi to his acolyte, and, addressing the student, "you can go without worries."

And the yeshiva *bocher*, his mind freed of qualms, goes home to his parents, his family, his village for the most important period of the year. To celebrate Roshaichounai (this is Russian Yiddish; in Hungary they said Rochhachono), Rosh Hashanah (in Hebrew), the new year, to pray during the frightful days when the Eternal weighs the souls, to pray in Yiddish at Yom Kipper or in Hebrew at Yom Kippur (in reality, the prayer is in Hebrew with a Yiddish accent), the day when one has to beg forgiveness from God for one's failings, forgive one's enemies—and ask them for forgiveness. He stays home even a bit longer. It feels so good to discuss things with his brothers and sisters, to see his friends again, to play with his nephews and nieces, to let himself be spoiled by his mother, to rest, to be able to linger in bed mornings after prayers in a heated room and to have plenty to eat—and to eat his mother's divine (oops, careful with this word! We are among religious people), let's say inimitable cooking, the best he has ever eaten in his whole life, his mother being the best cook, without doubt, of the commune, and perhaps even beyond (I'm not far from thinking the same thing about my own mother. And you?).

And then, then it's time to return to the yeshiva. Studies, the goal of life, await him. It's a bit hard on our student. His life away from home is not a bowl of cherries: he eats badly and little, sleeps in a cold room, has no friends, no distraction. . . . He studies. That's all. In order to gain understanding, and also to become a scholar, a man sought for his knowledge, his wisdom, his erudition, the soundness of his judgment.

The train pulls in too late in the evening for our young man to go to the rabbi to pick up his treasures. However, the next morning he rushes there right after morning prayers.

"*Shana tova*," says the student to the rabbi, wishing him a happy new year. The rabbi responds in the same manner; they tell each other plenty of good things, cordial, friendly ones—then the student broaches the main purpose of his visit: his things.

"What things?" Asks the holy man politely and a bit intrigued.

"But *Rebbe*, the things, my money, the candleholder, and other knickknacks that I entrusted you with before leaving! You well know that these were not knickknacks to me. It's all that I have. I have to go to the yeshiva, they are waiting for me there, please give them back to me."

"My dear, you must be mistaken. You've not left anything with me. Besides, you left without telling me good-bye and wishing me happy holidays, which surprised me and, I must confess, somewhat hurt my feelings."

The young man feels the ground shifting under his feet. Have I become mad? Do I have memory problems? Or has the rabbi gone crazy? The idea that his teacher would steal from him doesn't even enter his mind.

Nonetheless . . . the discussion takes forever, the young man reminds the rabbi of the precise circumstances of his handing over his things. The rabbi denies everything, claims he wasn't even in town that day. . . . Voices are raised, the student is at once ashamed for his teacher and angry at him. The rabbi begins to insult him, calls him a liar . . .

"But," says the *bocher*, "there was a witness to my handing these objects to you! The *shames*! You had him come into the room and even ordered him to testify if need be! Just call him!"

"As you wish—no problem."

And the rabbi calls the *shames*, who comes in right away.

"Yankel, did you see this young man give me . . ."

The student interrupts: "Money, which you carefully counted and noted, a candleholder, a ring, and a pocket watch. You were witness to my handing them over, in this very same room."

Yankel has seen nothing: "What are you saying? Are you mad? You need medical help. You handed nothing to the rabbi in my presence. And don't you dare call me a liar. I won't tolerate it, particularly not from—"

"Enough Yankel. This young man is hallucinating. It's useless to yell at him. Because," and the rabbi turns toward the young man, "I am not for a second suspecting you to try to get from me objects you have never owned. This would not be like you. I've known you for a long time and I have too good an opinion of you. Go in peace. Forget this incident. It never happened. And you Yankel, you can go. I forbid you to speak of this to anyone."

The student is feeling dizzy. "Lord, help me!" He has lost all his possessions, and worse, he has lost forever any trust he had for his teacher! He'll have to leave this yeshiva right away, leave the town. . . . But how to explain this to his parents, his friends?

He stands up and is about to leave the room without another word when the rabbi addresses him: "Wait a minute."

He opens a locked closet and in the most casual manner he pulls out the canvas bag, the object of the controversy. Under the young man's astounded eyes he empties its contents on the table: bills, coins, candleholder, ring, watch. . . . It's all there.

"Now you can see for yourself," says the rabbi to the student, "the sort of people I'm surrounded with!"

* * *

Written on the day I turned sixty-six and the day after Yom Kippur, on the twenty-third of September of 2007. Only fifty-four more years bis hundert zwanzig.[15]

15. [The literal meaning in Yiddish is "until one hundred and twenty," an expression meaning "May you live a long life." — TRANS.]

14

Of Strength (of Conviction)

This joke calls up a distant memory, that of the blue and white book-shaped piggy bank lying around in my grandparents' apartment after the war. It had been put there by a Zionist organization to help people go to Israel. (My father used to make the caustic comment: a Zionist is a Jew who is sending to Israel a second Jew with the money of a third one).

The birth of this text provoked a heated discussion with Karin. She felt that it was clearly and openly anti-Semitic. It shows Jews that are greedy, for whom money comes before anything else . . .

We are touching here upon the very essence of Jewish stories.

My wife's criticism would have been justified if the story had been told by someone else and from elsewhere. However, published here as told by myself in this context, it is no more objectionable than the other jokes in this book. Only Jews can—and have the right—to make fun of themselves. And they don't deprive themselves of it! (This is of course valid for all countries and nations).

Exaggeration, the over-the-top comic charge, prevents the story from being taken seriously, from being seen as anti-Semite.

True, the stories do feature some negative aspects of Jews, but always with indulgence, and these aspects are counterbalanced with positive ones.

Humor must be the dominating trait, and we laugh whether the story is about Jews, Corsicans, or Belgians, this without an ounce of meanness. We have to laugh at someone's expense, make fun of his or her foibles. It's superstition. It enables us to avoid being weighed down by these foibles in ourselves. It's a very human characteristic.

Almost all jokes, whether they be Jewish or not, play on the opposition between several subjects, and, most of the time, these form a duality. The wealthy and (or against) the poor, the smart one and the idiot (the smart one being very often stupid and the stupid one very often wise), the honest man and the thief (the thief being at times more honest than the "honest" man), the individual and society (or the group), the outward and the inner aspects (the visible and the hidden), the scholar and the illiterate, the brave and the coward . . . man and woman!

The following story is no exception to these rules.

Over the entrance of a New York bar there was a sign: "One hundred dollars reward to the person who succeeds in extracting one more drop from a lemon previously squeezed by our bartender."

Business was bad. The owner was hoping to attract new customers. Since there wasn't anything else he could rely on, he bet on the bartender. Not so much for his dexterity or his talents in making cocktails, since he had attended one, then another, and finally a third business school, all with good reputations, but from where he was kicked out for repeatedly being violent. So his drinks were and remained close to undrinkable. No, the boss was relying on the bartender's strength. His grip was famous in all of New York City's business schools.

And the owner was proven right: ever since the day he came up with the squeezed lemon contest, and put the sign over his door, the bar had never been empty. The group of regular customers had been supplemented by three new categories: musclemen, and even more by bragging loudmouths, and along with them, curious onlookers.

Biceps were on parade. Movers, truck drivers, longshoremen, boxers, wrestlers, weight lifters, shot put throwers, judokas, mafioso henchmen and other adepts of the martial arts, nightclub bouncers, amateur killers (professional soldiers) and professional ones (mafiosi hit men). Then also there were all those who wanted to take a shot, either because they were attracted to the game or by the prospect of money.

The owner was ecstatic. His most numerous customers were the curious onlookers who came to watch the show. The musclemen, after each failure, automatically swelled the ranks of the curious, which meant he still didn't lose their business! (There must be a marketing term to scientifically designate the concept I just mentioned).

The story would not be complete if I failed to mention that the bartender quickly asked for a raise—a raise that the boss, like all bosses deserving of the title—immediately and instinctively refused. His argument centered around the quality, that is the total absence of quality, of the drinks mixed by his employee, of the risks entailed by civil and professional responsibility that he, the bar owner, was incurring by letting his customers drink these liquids, of the opportunity he had offered the bartender, an unemployed student kicked out of every school, with the certitude of regular wages which would make it possible for him to start a family (a clumsy argument since being a father and husband was at the bottom of the list of his wishes and at the top of the list of his fears). At any rate, faced with the simple and logical argument that even the simplest-minded would have used, namely the threat of offering the competition his manual qualities, that of the palms of his hands and the strength of his fingers, the boss was forced to agree. He had no choice. He was aware that he was entirely dependent on his bartender; nay, his very survival depended on him. As for himself, he was only the owner-exploiter, profiting from the labor provided by a specialized worker (in a way, the definition of capitalism). His only role was limited to having come up with the idea for the product, to having brought in the initial investment, and to providing an adequate place of business. (Comrade Marx, what do you think of that? Are you pleased with me? But if you're pleased with me, it's because you've not kept abreast of the labor market: the labor provided has been for a long time less valued than the concept stated above.) In short, the barkeep accepted a raise proportional to the rise in profits of the bar. He readily agreed, because in addition being stupid, strong, and violent, the bartender was also lazy, so that the idea of looking for another job, another boss, showing his resume, negotiating, was already tiring him before the fact.

One beautiful day, beautiful because it was a horrible rainy and cold Sunday afternoon with no baseball match to watch, the crowd, having as its only choice TV shows or a live event, was pressed around the bar to enjoy the live one. Individuals and families had come from afar. They were lifting up children over the bar so that they could see. Bets were taken on whether a certain bodybuilder could or could not beat the bartender. So it was on a blessed Sunday when the crowd was denser than ever that a short, scrawny guy elbowing his way and stepping on toes made it to the bar.

"'Let me try," he said to the bartender.

At first no one heard him in the din. He had to repeat his demand two, three times, louder and louder, before it reached the barkeep's and the rest of the crowd's ears.

There was general consternation, followed by an explosion of glee and laughter.

"Hey, have you ever seen yourself in the mirror, ha ha, you'll have to take off your tie, and how are you going to be able to even lift the lemon," etc.

One has to say that the proposition was absurd. The individual in question was less than five foot five, with a prominent belly (not very big, but considering the rest of him being so skinny, his stomach looked like a regular pot belly), and the shoulders of his small jacket couldn't hide how thin his shoulders actually were. And then his general appearance: a tired striped shirt, a tie knotted very small and tight, accordion-like crumpled pants, and a pair of shoes ageless, devoid of fashion, destination, future, and barely in possession of a shabby past. A myopic's eyeglasses with an old steel frame added the missing aesthetic touch.

Numerous people had already taken up the barkeep's challenge without anyone able to win the hundred dollars. But never, never ever had any of the competitors presented this sort of image, one of insignificance, grayness, weakness.

The bartender and his boss were pretty annoyed. What's the use? This little guy will make the crowd leave, since there won't be any show. The result being known in advance, there will be nothing to see.

But the laws are strict. It is forbidden to break the rules of a public competition.

Disgusted, the barkeep takes a lemon, he wonders for a moment whether he should squeeze it with his weaker hand, his left one, and then, who cares, he's too tired to even create a minievent. So he pours a gin and tonic in a glass—the standard drink when the customer hasn't requested another kind—then squeezes the lemon over the glass. He actually squashes it; it even appears that all of a sudden he takes pleasure in humiliating this . . . what, this worm, this loser who doesn't know what to do with his Sundays; he flattens the citrus, empties it of all its juice, totally dries it up . . . then hands it over to the customer while pushing the glass under his nose.

The little guy doesn't go for the musclemen's usual showmanship. He doesn't take off his jacket, doesn't pull up his sleeves, doesn't even push his hat up on his forehead. He casually and totally naturally grabs the lemon with his right hand, the lemon that is as flat as a sheet of paper, and effortlessly squeezes it, without his face showing any strain, with the air of someone performing a boring, everyday task.

Six fat drops fall, one after another, into his glass.

Silence, there's an indescribable silence. One can't even hear anyone breathing.

It's something never seen. A kind of miracle.

The silence lasts. The customer calmly drinks his lemon gin and tonic, then just as calmly but with a determined mien, asks for his hundred dollars.

The bartender is astounded. Once recovered from his astonishment, he tries to compose himself. To be beaten by Sugar Ray Robinson, OK. By Muhammad Ali, that's still all right. By a longshoreman, that's acceptable. Well, it was going to happen one day, even though that day was getting increasingly problematical, given his constant training of his right hand. But to be beaten, to be ridiculed, yes, ri-diculed, by this puny twerp, no way!

He looks in desperation toward the owner, who opens up his cash register drawer and hands over a one-hundred-dollar bill to the victor.

Then, suddenly the silence breaks into a thousand pieces. The sound of the cash register opens up the sluices of comments, stories, exclamations, questions, interpellations, wonderings, yells, laughter, teasing, admiring whistles.

Who is this guy? He has never been seen in the neighborhood—no one knows him—is he from New York, is he American? He is obvious-ly too scrawny to practice any of the professions requiring physical strength such as mover, cop, sport, body guard. . . . So whence comes his unusual strength? Is he a member of the secret service? Or he has a ploy, he must have cheated. . . . Where does he train? In which club? Does he have a sponsor?

The boss is not unhappy. First this defeat will tamper his Herculean barkeep's posturing, and since the event is exceptional, the whole town will be abuzz. Newspapers will report on it.

"Who are you sir?" he asks the mysterious customer. "What is your profession that it gives you so much strength? How were you able to extract several drops from a totally dry lemon?"

The man calmly takes the hundred-dollar bill, carefully folds it, and puts it in his wallet before answering in a modest and indifferent tone of voice: "I am a fund-raiser for the Unified Jewish Appeal."

15

In English in the Text

Azesponemski, Jeffrey Glen George Azesponemski, is involved in a lawsuit. For goodness' sake, how come this man who had been at the top of his class, with his eyeglasses, pomaded hair, shave so close as to make his skin pink, smelling of pink roses, three-piece-suit-pristine-shirt-necktie-cufflinks is involved in lawsuits? What is he accused of? What has he done? It's always suspect—there's no smoke without fire—where does he come from—those foreigners always have problems. If he makes such a good living, why is he still living in Brooklyn?

In fact, Azesponemski is the plaintiff. He got stuck in an inextricable morass from having lent the down payment to one of his cousins (an Ashkenazi-type cousin) to help him buy an apartment with the money that a company belonging to this cousin was supposed to deposit—but in the meanwhile the company instead of making a deposit had incurred a debit and declared itself broke, and the cousin, having already deposited his four kids, wife and his parents in the apartment, . . . Should I keep going? I better simplify: Azesponemski wants to recover his down payment. The law is on his side. But the seller doesn't want to return it. The law is also on the seller's side. Thus Azesponemski is suing the seller . . . well let's skip it, it's getting too complicated. Even Azesponemski himself is getting lost in it. As for the others, no need to even mention their confusion. Only the lawyers see clearly. They are happy, as always. They tap each other on the back and laugh very loud, in private, that is. If you can't figure out why, just come to see me after the session. I'll explain it to you.

So, here we are, in front of the district court in Brooklyn. On my left, the lawyer of the claimant and that of the cousin. Behind them, Azesponemski and his cousin. On my right, the lawyer of the one who refuses to give back the money. Facing them is the judge. On his left the court clerk, on his right a somewhat sad-looking man (digression: as if the others were happy!), the interpreter.

The session begins, or rather it would begin, except that Azesponemski jumps up from his seat and points a trembling and accusing finger toward the interpreter.

"Your Honor, what is it that I'm seeing? An interpreter? I am deeply shocked, insulted. I feel that the interpreter's presence is an allusion, an insinuation, an intolerable contempt, a whiff of anti-Semitism and a fetid smell of racism and of xenophobia, all in flagrant breech of our constitution. Of course I will take this up with the appropriate judicial authorities. I have to insist on the fact that I was born in this country, in this city, Your Honor, and even if this hadn't been so, I am a US citizen. At home with my parents we only spoke English, I attended a nursery school reserved for whites three blocks from here, I went to a private elementary school in the same street, I attended high school in this same state, a very selective establishment with a sterling reputation of which I don't wish to brag, but I nonetheless have to mention that then I studied in London. I hold a degree from the London Business School, where, according to the latest news, the teaching is done in English, and also a degree from MIT. Moreover, I wish the clerk to note that I am married to an American, a white one, Protestant, her family originating from Scotland, and who, like all my children, was born in this country. At home we speak English, and only English—so what is the meaning of this nonsense? An interpreter? Your Honor, I energetically and solemnly protest the interpreter's presence. I demand that he immediately leave the courtroom."

The old judge listens to this monologue impassively, greets the attacks serenely, and calmly waits for Azesponemski, shaking under the sway of emotion, to sit down. The judge then turns toward the interpreter and asks him in Yiddish: "What did he say?"

16

A Witz *for All Seasons*

My cousin Tomi, three years older than me, who after having left tragic Hungary for rainy Great Britain, is now enjoying a happy retirement in the sunny Cévennes in France, liked to tell stories. It must run in our family. It's from him that I learned the Hungarian expression alapvicc, *"a basic* witz,*" when we were still Hungarian kids, without for a second imagining that Tomi would one day be an English management consultant, and I a Swiss and then French publisher.* Alap *means "basic, foundation";* alapvicc *means a* witz *that is required knowledge as it is part and parcel of a cultured man (from Budapest, of course) and which can serve as a basis for everyday life. It represents deep wisdom, folk wisdom that can be cited and applied to numerous occasions, and which forms the basis of many other stories. It's a fundamental* witz, *in a way a root-*witz.

So here it is, very basic. A witz *known to all, even you. And if this isn't the case, try it and you'll see the many uses you'll have for it. You're going to thank me.*

Moshe owes one thousand dollars to Shlomo. Why dollars? Why not zlotys, forints, leis, rubles, dinars, or even after all CFA francs? Well yes, why not? Let say that our heroes, who for once I won't name Kohn and Grün, live, how lucky can they be, in the country of all dreams, in the United States of America. And consequently, they are no longer called Moshe and Shlomo, after all we are no longer in the old country: they call themselves Derek and Clint. Is that agreeable to you, American cousins? And don't tell me that no Jew would answer to these goy names, because first it isn't true—every one knows that your children will respond when they feel like it to the silliest names—and second, do I have to answer you? Don't worry, the punch line will not be American in spite of the names. It will be universal (we are dealing here with the *alapvicc* of all *alapvicc*).

So we come back to our poor, really poor, Derek, who is not able to give back the thousand dollars he had recklessly borrowed from Clint and which the latter had even more recklessly lent him. Derek was supposed to pay back the money on December first and now it's already the night of November 30. The year is of no import—I've told you that the story is timeless and "polytopic" (this later is a Yiddish-sounding word I just invented by combining *poly*, meaning "numerous," and *topos*, meaning "place").

As a result Derek can't sleep. He knows that Clint expects his money the next day, that he really needs it, and that he, Derek, won't be able to give it back to him because he doesn't have it. He doesn't have a dime. Let's not attempt an explanation; let's not look for one. We are in the country of unlimited possibilities, where, if someone is poor, it can only be his or her fault. Insurance companies have eliminated chance and fate.

Derek turns in his bed, drinks a sip of water, scratches, coughs, plumps his pillow, looks at the glowing face of his watch, then he gets up, drags himself to the kitchen, fills his glass with fresh water, goes to the bathroom, flushes . . . in short, the usual nocturnal activities of someone who has trouble sleeping but is not used to it. Insomniacs don't behave that way. They have their own habits: newspapers, books, radio, work, TV. There are even some that step outside, make a tour of the yard. You can often read their eyewitness accounts in the newspapers on the murders and robberies they chanced to witness during the night.

Not only is poor Derek unable to sleep, he is keeping his dear Sharon, his cosufferer (his sympathizer, from *syn* meaning "with" and *pathos* meaning "suffering," *mitleidende*), from sleeping as well. It's obvious that all these activities wake Sharon up. We might even wonder if all these mini-noises, aimed at not disturbing anyone, are in reality aimed at waking up the cosleeper (*mitschlafende*) so as to be able to share boredom, temporary insomnia, indigestion, the beginning of the flu, pain, distress, despair.

Thus Sharon is up. She looks at the clock, drinks some water, goes to the bathroom, flushes—it seems women behave pretty much in a manly manner when confronted with the serious moments of life. Unless, it's the opposite.

"Why aren't you sleeping, Derek?" She asks while yawning, annoyed, tired.

"I'm not sleeping because I can't fall asleep," answers Derek in a very Cartesian mode.

"Why is that?"

Up till then the play of questions and answers had been pretty clear and you could even say, classical. It's now that the sentence that will save the conversation from banality is uttered.

"I owe a thousand dollars [he probably actually said "a thousand bucks"—here a note at the bottom of the page would say: "In English in the original," which gives an authentic cachet to the text and enables the author to shine with little effort], I owe a thousand dollars to Clint."

"So?" asks his bed companion.

"I don't have it," says Derek.

"I know," says Sharon.

"What you don't know, because you don't always know everything [on whom else can he take things out at three AM if not his wife? All the more so that they are alone at home, so there are no other victims in sight), it's that I have to return his dough on December first. And this is it, since midnight, it's already December 1. And that in five or six hours, this bastard Clint will wait for me to come with the money. And I don't know what to do. And it's going to go badly. So, you-the-all-knowing-one, do you have some idea? A good one for a change? Where can we find a thousand bucks at three AM? And even at nine AM? There's nothing left we can sell. No more carpets, paintings, no more valuable books, no more jewels. So? I'm listening."

As if it was Sharon's fault. Well, it is her fault. Derek had to borrow money because Sharon is a spendthrift.

"Go back to bed, I'm going to take care of it," says Sharon.

"Yes? I'd like to know how."

They are now both wide awake. It no longer feels like the middle of the night, but high noon. They are awake, lively, talkative.

Sharon pulls open the bedroom drapes, opens the window.

"You've gone mad? What's got into you? We're freezing! This is not July! And it's too bad because then I still would have five months to find the money."

Sharon, cool as a cucumber, opens the windows wide and yells into the night:

"Shlooooooomoooo! Shlooooooomoooo!" calls Sharon, cleaving the thick glass of night.

One can hear a window opening at the other side of the street. It's Lisa, Clint's wife, wearing lace-edged pink jammies.

"What the matter Sharon? Do you know what time it is! Something serious?"

"Moshe owes a thousand dollars to Clint," yells Sharon at the top of her lungs. Derek hides under the comforter, but he would rather hide under the ground, ten feet under, from shame. He's going to move the next day, that's for sure. Perhaps without Sharon even.

Lisa answers, yelling a bit less loudly but yelling nonetheless, that she is aware of it, and that it's today that Derek is supposed to pay back the money. They are waiting for it and really need it. To the small bedside lamp that was already lit on the other side of the street at Lisa's now is added the bigger light of a chandelier. Thus Clint is also awake and is listening to the conversation. Other lights are turning on here and there in the street.

"Well, Derek has no money. He can't give back your thousand dollars," yells Sharon. Then she noisily closes the window, pulls the curtains shut, and goes back to bed next to Derek, who feels more dead than alive.

"There. Now you can sleep in peace," she says. "Now it's him who isn't sleeping."

∗ ∗ ∗

I told you: a basic witz, good for all of life's events.

Of Jews and of Others

This is a French story and I'm not sure that it would be understood elsewhere, for instance in the US or in Eastern Europe. I'm not going to comment on it; I'm not going to explain it. Let readers figure it out for themselves. Just a note: in France all Jews from North Africa are referred to as Shepardi instead of limiting the term to Jews whose ancestors came from Spain. Nowadays they form the majority among the people who were repatriated after decolonization. A Moroccan Jew friend of mine liked to tease me with the joke "You know, Adam, why we appreciate you so much? Because Ashkenazi are the Jew's best friends."

A young Parisian woman, sexy, even beautiful, cultured, intelligent (let's not confuse culture with intelligence!), holding an excellent job, and everything positive you can imagine, is bringing her parents to despair. She is twenty-nine years old and she is not only not yet married, but she doesn't even have a prospect. And she is no one's prospect either! You can imagine Mr. and Mrs. Peinlichnik's despair. They are not going to have grandchildren—what could be worse! The fact that the beautiful Sarah could get married and have marvelous children without problem till she's forty doesn't bring them the least bit of consolation. They want to see her married—now! Now, right away! Not in ten years! Where will we be in ten years? My God, Rachel, where will we be (no question mark here. It's not a question, it's a declaration. Mr. Peinlichnik *knows* where he will be in ten years. Even though he's only fifty-four. No matter. He knows. Like he knows the rest, because Mr. Peinlichnik is like many of your acquaintances: he knows everything).

The accused is convoked. What are you doing? What are you doing with your time? You think that by working night and day (Sarah is head engineer for a pharmaceutical laboratory) you'll find a husband? To be still single, virgin (Sarah has trouble stifling a smile at that point), at twenty-nine! Your mother was eighteen when we got married, yes missy! What's the use of all your degrees? They're not asking you for a diploma to give birth to a child (another exclamation mark; we need one at the end of each statement to clearly show the passionate-impassioned aspect of the conversation—what conversation? You call this monologue a conversation?)! And your work, I'm going to tell you what I think about it: it keeps you from living! From going out, meeting people, young people, linking up . . . in short, you've perfectly understood me. You just have to change jobs, find some work that is less demanding, that leaves you free time, that let's you breathe! Mademoiselle gets home at nine PM, takes a bath, makes herself a miserable dinner that she eats alone, reads the paper—which she can't even finish because she's so tired she's falling asleep over it. Is that a life? Instead of having three, four, adorable little ones running pulling at your skirt? My grandmother had thirteen kids, one of which was my mother. I know, it was in Poland, another century. Still. My tailor grandfather didn't earn half, what am I saying, a tenth, of what you're making and provided for thirteen children and a wife, a whole household! No, I'm not saying you should have thirteen children. Anyway, it's too late for that. But two! Make us at least two, for the love of God! Oh, all of a sudden I have an idea: put an ad in the paper!

Sarah, we have to admit, is tired of this perennial conversation. It has been the topic every Friday evening when she comes to have dinner with her parents. She doesn't really listen, and yet . . . she does feel a bit alone. It's true, she isn't in a relationship with anyone. One for life, well after all, why not? Of course she knows lots of people, she went to the university, then she held several positions. . . . She even had several intense affairs, with young men who were not bad at all. Her parents didn't know a thing. What would have been the use? And at the last minute, or not at the last one, but just at one moment, it no longer worked. Sometimes it was her fault, sometimes the other's.

Maybe Daddy is right. After all, meeting someone in a lab is not less due to chance than a response to an ad. On the contrary!

So she agrees.

"OK, Papa. All right. Tomorrow I'll put an ad in the paper. What newspaper do you prefer?"

It's the wrong question, the one she shouldn't have asked.

There's a debate. First: let's put the ad in an Israeli paper—but, wait, Sarah then would go live in Israel along with the grandchildren, and that was not the goal. Next, an English-language paper. Here the issue is not the same, because many French people read English papers and English or American Jews living in France might see the ad. Etc., etc. "So the ad? In a Jewish paper? However . . ."

Sarah understands her mistake of asking about the paper. She decides that this journalistic debate has lasted long enough.

"Papa, I'll see. I'll ask my girlfriends."

And that was it.

Time passes. Mr. Peinlichnik is on pins and needles, and yet he doesn't ask any question. He doesn't dare. And Sarah doesn't make things any easier. She acts as if nothing happened, as if there were no enormous question and enormous wait hanging in the air.

And then, one day, approximately two months after the famous discussion, Mr. Peinlichnik can't stand it anymore. One Friday he bursts out, "So, you've said nothing about the responses you got. What is the meaning of your silence? How many? From where, from whom? Any interesting responses? So tell!"

Sarah looks at her parents, her dear parents and says (with what tone? I don't know, I wasn't there, but it might have gone from the defiant to the depressed and passed by the hilarious or the indifferent): "No response, zero, nada from nada."

"How can that be?" Exclaims her incredulous father. "No response? No one wants to meet a girl like you? The world is going to hell in a hand basket! You're so beautiful, have a degree, good financial situation. . . . Wake me up! I'm hallucinating! For the love of God, what did you put in this miserable ad that no one, no, I'm hallucinating, no one, not a one gave you a response?"

"Only banalities and conventionalities, papa," replies Sarah.

"But still? Tell it to me word for word."

"I've written exactly the following: 'Young Jewish woman from a good family, twenty-nine years old, with a degree, speaking three languages, loves children, seeks to meet for dating and possibly more if compatible, a young, cultured Shepardi or an optimistic Ashkenazi.'"

18

Di Ganef, Di Willst Davenen!

*My maternal grandparents lived three buildings away from the largest syna-
gogue of Budapest (that's certain), of Hungary (that's absolutely incontestable),
of Europe (that remains to be proven), of the world (surely not), that of Dohány
Street, which had been built on the spot where the house where Theodore Herzl
was born once stood. My pious maternal grandmother, the mother of my beloved
Communist and atheist mother, went there every Saturday accompanied by myself (when I was six or seven years old and slept at her house) and by my atheist
grandfather's taunts. We would seat ourselves on the balcony, in the women's
section. I remember an enormous place, dark, mysterious and empty. This wasn't
the case during the great holy days, when Yom Kippur Yids shoved each other
for space. (I don't need to tell you again, dear faithful and friendly listeners, the
widespread and shameful description of this illness.)*

*I had meant to call this story Di ganef, di willst benshen—which didn't
correspond to the content. The mistake was due to my little knowledge of Yiddish. Since then, I learned that benshen means to say the blessing, usually after
meals. The word is of French origin: it comes from bénir.*[16] *Davenen, in contrast,
means praying in general.*

*Well, I already knew this joke when still a kid in Hungary; later, in Paris, I
told it to the doctor Claude W., who then gave me another version, another ending. I adopted it on the spot; it was better than the one I had been familiar with.*

*This is how stories transform, evolve, live. Your turn to play, if you feel like
it. This story, like all the others in this book, is yours. Make good use of it; that
is, change it as you fancy, and don't let it die.*

---

16. ["To bless" in English. — TRANS.]

It's Yom Kippur. The Dohány Street synagogue in Budapest is filled
to bursting. Even the sidewalk in front of the building is dense with
people. There's no way to get through. The crowd is jostling the more
so because the end of the service is near, and no Jew, believer or not,
wants to miss the sound of the shofar.

It's then that Kohn shows up, out of breath, beside himself. He
visibly has been running—something strongly advised against on
the day of great forgiveness, when custom and even the Law require
that you spend the day at the synagogue, at looking into yourself, at
scrutinizing your conscience, at fasting and praying, and particularly
not at stressing, running, being agitated, filled with all manner of
concerns. The only authorized worries belong to the moral and spiri-
tual plane, but Kohn's are obviously of a temporal nature. He is late
for this holy day, just as he is late always and everywhere—this since
the dawn of time.

And like all of those who deep down know they're in the wrong,
while on the surface they resent everyone, Kohn is filled with a guilty
aggressiveness, doubly guilty considering the importance of this day.
He elbows his way through the crowd so as to make it to the *Schul* door
no matter what. He reaches it with great effort. That day, when you
must forgive your enemies and beg forgiveness from those you have
wronged, Kohn distributes large quantities of various blows, from
the elbow, the knee, the heel. And he gets as many as he gives, along
with insults and punches.

So he gets there. Here he is, after half an hour of one-hundred-per-
cent Israelite hand-to-hand combat (because he was only squashing
Jewish feet, and was sticking his elbows exclusively in Jewish ribs),
in front of the main entry to the synagogue. An entry barred by the
imposing stature of the *shames*.

"Your ticket?" he asks Kohn.

Kohn has not reserved a place. Like every year, like always, like
never.

"I see. You can't go in without a reserved place. I have my orders.
What do you think the community lives from? It lives from gifts—and
I don't think that you give often—and places bought for the great holy
days. I have to mention that in the communities of the provinces,

when there still are Jews, they are competing for offering to pay the highest price for a place. While you, who call yourself a Jew, you don't even want to pay one forint."

"Yes, but—" says Kohn.

"There's no yes but. Besides, can't you see that the synagogue is filled to the bursting point, that there is no more room, neither seated nor standing?"

"I absolutely have to find my uncle Grün Jakab to give him an extremely important message. He's seated all the way up front. I know, he told me."

"No," says the *shames*. "You can't go."

"I won't stay, I promise. I'll just transmit the message to my uncle Jakab and I'll come back. I will not clutter the ranks."

"Forget it. I can't let you enter. On the one hand you don't have a ticket, and on the other there's no more room."

Kohn has a logical mind. "I don't understand. On the one hand . . . on the other. . . . Would you let me in if I had a ticket?"

"Stop your pilpul already! I told you there's not a single place left."

Kohn feels triumphant. He feels he was right not to reserve a place, since the synagogue is full! So the first obstacle has been overcome, but there's still the problem of lack of space.

"But I'm telling you I'm not staying. I'm only going and coming. As soon as I tell my uncle what I have to tell him, I'll be back. Anyway, you'll see me. And if you don't see me coming back, come and get me. Besides, since the synagogue is full, I can't imagine where I could stay."

The *shames* takes a good look for a long time at the little Kohn, mumbling, agitated, convincing, sputtering, pitching, and felt sorry for him. After all it's a day, *the* day of the year, when you have to love your fellow human being.

He says to him: "All right, go find your uncle. But don't let me catch you trying to pray!"

* * *

The other version, mine but not as good, ended with: Di ganef, di willst davenen! *"You dishonest person—you want to pray!*

Assimilation

On the day my cousin Tomi of London, the successful English management consultant, the Hungarian cousin from Budapest I spoke of earlier, had come to visit us in Paris for the first time, wearing his British club necktie (both being British, that is the necktie and the club), his pipe filled with British tobacco, and his British accent, I immediately thought of the following anecdote.

At the time when Europe began to sink into miasmic waters, when the ignominious tip of the first anti-Jewish laws began to grow out of this fetid swamp, when the first *numerus clausus* were decreed in the 1930s, Salomon Hajsvasser, a very poor Talmudic student from a yeshiva from "over there," decided to migrate to Great Britain. In his mind, England was the last stronghold of individual liberty, a solid and unbreakable democratic rock in the raging ocean of hateful and inhumane dictatorships of whose emergence he had become aware. (Well, it's totally true. As much as my father was suspicious of the frivolity of Romance countries, of Gallic immorality, of Germanic rigidity, he idolized British democracy. How many times did I hear him quote "My home is my castle"?[17] And if this is still more or less true today, we can wonder, for how long?)

Hajsvasser thus decided to go to England, and Great Britain had no objections to letting Hajsvasser come in. The young Jew was studious, intelligent, and ambitious. "He wanted to make it,"[18] they used to say in American English (do they still say it, or has it been replaced by a more hip expression?). He was angry first at the Central European

17. [In English in the original. — TRANS.]
18. [In English in the original. — TRANS.]

country that he had just left, and he did want to make it. He wanted
to conquer the world, like others, those very often Jewish legendary
characters who had left the same regions in the same or worse circumstances and then found fabulous success in film, the press, or photog-
raphy. Like the one who traveled on foot through Europe, or that other
who began as a street newspaper seller in New York and ended up a
newspaper magnate, a fabulously wealthy and feared producer in Hollywood, a genius film director, and ennobled by the queen in London.

Hajsvasser wanted nothing less. In which field? He didn't care. He
had decided to give up religion, Judaism, his Talmudic studies, his
past, his country, his parents, all of his history. He even killed God.
To live for the present—and the future! To become wealthy (first and
foremost), and also recognized and admired. And then as fringe benefit, to be surrounded by ravishing, exotic, and mysterious women,
take fabulous journeys in unknown regions, and work at a profession
that would not be too taxing and of course that would make him rich.

In contrast to many of his compatriots and fellow Jews, he did not
content himself with dreams and sighs. He did what he had to do to
become wealthy, etc. (see above). Let us not search, not dwell deeper,
into the ways he used to succeed. Was it Balzac who wrote that a crime
hides behind every financial success? I told you, he even killed God.
Let us spare him however from Cocteau's famous quip: "He made it,
but in what state!" No, that would be unfair. Even at the height of his
success, Hajsvasser looked good and sported the smile of a satiated
carnivore.

In what field did he make his fortune? Certainly not as a rabbi;
you figured that out. But who knows his path to fortune today? And
what import could it have? It happened decades and decades ago; war,
decolonization, a groundswell of what?—of everything—pushed and
pulled it all under. It was another world. Hajsvasser was a prehistoric
animal. Was he admired? And yet at the time everything he touched
turned to gold, pounds sterling, dollars. And how! Newspapers could
have featured a special column "Hajsvasser"; "Mr. Hajsvasser inaugu-
rates the new . . . the biggest . . . the most beautiful . . . his second . . ."
and so on. As for women, the same thing. "Mr. Hajsvasser with Miss X
at the ball of . . . , with Baroness Y at the reception held by Mr. and Mrs.

Z, . . . with the actress AB on his yacht *Emperor* in the Pacific ocean," and more and even more! (We must notice that he was married—but who cares?)

Toward the end of the year 1948, Hajsvasser received a letter from his cousin Isi Überhohem, from the old country. A letter in the language of the old country (no, no, it wasn't Norwegian, it was Yiddish). Isi was telling him in the most serious, brief, and mysterious words that he had been granted authorization to go to Great Britain, and that he thus was going to have the pleasure of seeing again his cousin whom he had not seen for fifteen years. Incidentally, he noted that barring contrary notice, he planned to live with him during his stay. Isi wasn't asking for any response. He also communicated, in case of need, the exact day and time of arrival of his train.

Hajsvasser understood that he had no choice. He had to pick up Isi at the station (will I recognize him?) And he had to put him up (for how long?). Family ties and the situation in Eastern European countries didn't allow him to refuse. You can't donate to all the charities helping Jews on the other side of the Iron Curtain, sign countless petitions all day and all newspaper long, proclaim your solidarity at all the dinner parties in town, and then fail to help on the first real occasion. (In fact, you can. It's a proven fact. It's easier for a rich man to give money than to have breakfast with a relative from *over there*. Money costs the least).

So here is the Lubitsch style scene: the Rolls-Royce Silver Shadow glides noiselessly in front of Victoria Station. An English gentleman with a bowler hat comes out, his moustache vaguely military in form, his face closely shaved, scented with *vetiver*, camel hair coat, carnation in his lapel, cream-colored gloves, striped pants, black lacquer shoes. The chauffeur remains at the wheel. The gentleman is two minutes ahead of the train, two minutes that allow him to be right on the spot next to the locomotive at the very instant the train pulls into the station.

Hajsvasser has no trouble recognizing his cousin in the flood of travelers, most of them French, since the train had left from Paris, the transit point from Eastern Europe. Cousin Überhohem couldn't be confused with anyone: dressed in the Eastern European Communist formal chic style, a London tramp would have been offended to be compared to him. There is no pleasure in describing it. It is more pleasant, more enjoyable, for a positive being like myself to describe the appearance of a gentleman of the City. Everything on Überhohem screamed of the East: the cut of the suit, the material, the suitcase, the manner of carrying his coat, the way of moving, of speaking, of looking for his cousin, the inarticulate exclamation when the latter let himself be known by a discreet hand gesture.

There's no point in wasting time describing Überhohem's many surprises, from the way his cousin was dressed, then the chauffeur rushing to take his suitcase, then the city of London. . . . We will not give Überhohem's clinical details of his arrival in front of Red Oak Mansion, Hajsvasser's palatial town house (heart attack), climbing the marble steps (cerebral stroke), the foyer (apoplectic attack) and the suite assigned to him (aneurism burst).

"Make yourself at home," says Hajsvasser in Oxford Yiddish. "Take a pleasant bath, *old chap*—you must be tired after your long trip—and come to join us in the library for a nice cup of tea. My wife will be very happy; she can't wait to meet you."

Überhohem had wanted to see Hajsvasser's wife right away and talk to his cousin. He was astonished, flabbergasted, overwhelmed. He wanted the complete story, explanations, everything. However, the butler was already running the water for his bath and opening his suitcase with disgusted fingers. Überhohem felt he had to obey.

As soon as the bath had been expedited, as soon as he had soaped, wiped, dressed, the whole at the speed of light, Isi rushed to the library, or rather would have rushed if he had found it. He had to open many doors before the butler caught up with him and led him to the fire lit in the fireplace, the tea already served, Hajsvasser ensconced in an armchair, wearing a smoking jacket, smoking his pipe, and facing Lady Hajsvasser on the couch. Can we describe her? No we can't. How boring! What? The description, just the description. An English-woman like they knew how to manufacture at the time in England, and only in England. A unique model, patented, registered. Including everything: the hairdo, the posture, the way of holding the teacup, the afternoon dress, the stockings, the shoes, the accent, the *shake hand*, the *Britannia rules the seas*, the *God save the Queen*, and others, the *It's a long way to Tipperary.* We sure are far, very far, from the other Europe, the Central one.

After the medics again revive Überhohem, and before he can ask any questions, and God knows he has plenty, he has to talk about the political situation in his country so as to make Hajsvasser understand that he is on a business trip, charged with buying some things of no interest to Hajsvasser, and that he couldn't have mentioned this in his letter. And that it is the special services in Paris that had found his cousin's address in London. And that he is only going to stay a short week with them.

At last, it was Überhohem's turn to ask questions.

How to start? With what question? With the extraordinary and rapid road taken by Hajsvasser, spanning the fifteen years between the destitute emigrant, the Talmudic student, the Jew in rags speaking only Yiddish that Überhohem had accompanied to the station, and the quasi-lord who had come to pick him up at Victoria Station??? Or instead: !!!

In fact there is a question burning on Überhohem's lips, one more important than the story of Hajsvasser's exploits and heroic trajectory, the essential question, the only one of true interest, the one giving meaning to life: "Tell me, Salomon, are you happy?"

There's a long, a very long, silence. Hajsvasser draws on his pipe, gazes at the tobacco turning red, pokes the fire in the fireplace, emits a deep sigh, a very deep and true sigh, before answering: "Happy? Isi, you're asking me if I am happy? How could I be, when we're about to lose India?"

There is another version of the story you've just heard, and now that I'm done telling it, I'm beginning to think that I prefer it. At any rate, I'm not going to start over. I'm much too lazy and this is not a school assignment. The other version is the poorer one:

Hajsvasser, far from having become a millionaire, very far from having succeeded, barely gets by in London, living on the edge of homelessness and beggary. One day quite accidentally, he meets his cousin Überhohem in the street. They talk, each tells his story. Überhohem has just arrived from *over there*; Hajsvasser, dressed in clothes nearing rag status, has lived in London for more than fifteen years. Überhohem is surprised by his cousin's misery, his failure, but he doesn't say anything. He only asks him: "Say, Salomon, are you happy here?"

And Hajsvasser's reply is the same as in the other version, but here it is more striking and more moving: "Happy? Isi, you're asking me if I'm happy? How could I be, since we're about to lose India?"

Regardless of the version you prefer, I would like to continue the story. It can work just as well with either versions.

The two cousins are walking around in London. Salomon, who is very familiar with the city, *his* city, is proud to show it to his cousin Isi. This latter is obviously very impressed. Who wouldn't be, coming from the devastated countries of Eastern Europe with their cities and souls in ruin? Salomon shows him enormous monuments, impressive all-white palaces, shops filled with appetizing and exciting merchandise, frenetic traffic, red buses as tall as houses, the underground *tube*, Britishers' orderly and courteous interactions, unarmed *bobbies*. He's so proud, our Salomon, and as he listens to his cousin's sincere exclamations, he feels as if he were the architect, the city planner, even the main tenant, the owner!

"Ah yes," says Isi with a sigh, "it's not Grodno!"

"Well no," replies Salomon. "This is an immense city, as big as a whole country. How many people are there in Grodno?"

He asks the question as if he hadn't come from Grodno himself, as if he hadn't been born there, as if he hadn't lived for many long years in the house next to that of Isi's parents—as if he didn't know the town by heart, with his eyes closed, at night, in his sleep, at all times of the day, every day . . .

"Twenty thousand."

"And how many Jews?"

"About fifteen thousand."

"And what are the others doing?"

"They're policeman, firemen, street sweepers, tax collectors, bureaucrats . . ."

Salomon is lost in reflection. He doesn't remember, didn't know these figures.

Then Isi Überhohem turns toward Salomon Hajsvasser and asks him: "And in London, how many inhabitants?"

"I'm not exactly sure. Perhaps two million."

Isi is very impressed. "What a big city! And how many Jews out of these two million?"

"Oh, I don't really know, many, maybe one hundred thousand."

Isi is flabbergasted. "What? One hundred thousand? Do you really need so many policemen, firemen, street sweepers, and tax collectors?"

20

You Can't Escape Your Fate

Again a political story. An old story dating from the time of my childhood, even though it was told to me recently by a vacation neighbor, in a Hungarian resort on the shore of the Danube, to serve as illustration for 2007 news. This story is history—but unfortunately it's timeless and still lives today. All Eastern Europeans in my age group will understand it without a dictionary, but the others will need a translation.

Present-day news: on Sunday, July 8, 2007, a Gay Pride parade was held in Budapest. The Hungarian extreme right wing attacked and seriously wounded many gay participants while hurling anti-Semitic slogans at them: "A buzik a Dunába, a zsidók meg utána" ("Throw the faggots in the Danube, and then the Jews"). This slogan alludes to the events of January 1945, when the Hungarian Nazis, the Arrow Cross, threw Jews into the Danube in Budapest. (Remember to never tell the following as a joke: "One must hang all Jews and cyclists." There will always be someone among your friends to ask: why the cyclists?)

This is the history part: from 1949 till the fall of the Berlin wall in 1989, people were not allowed to leave any of the countries of the Communist block, the countries occupied by the Soviet army. Until 1956, one could not travel abroad at all, and that applied even to travel between "brother countries." Hungarians, Czechs, Russians, Bulgarians didn't even have passports, and the borders were hermetically closed. There were barbed wire fences, no man's lands, observation towers, dogs, armed border guards. It's barely conceivable nowadays.

A bit of relaxation of these rules began in 1956, then more markedly in 1962.

Nonetheless during the first month of the Communist takeover in Hungary, a certain number of Hungarians tried to enter the West illegally through Hungary's only Western border, the Austrian one. These clandestine emigrants were called

disszidensek, "dissidents," and the act of migrating illegally, disszidálni, a
verb that is not translatable yet very understandable.

During the last month of 1949, Kohn *bácsi*, uncle Kohn (in the generic sense of "uncle" applied to most old men), old man Kohn got
caught by Hungarian border guards during his night escape attempt
from Hungary to Austria (it's no longer necessary to introduce Kohn.
You're already acquainted with him. And why "old man Kohn?" Because that's the way they said it. Old Kohn, implying one who survived
everything, knew everything, saw everything and experienced everything—which happens often in life, and always in jokes. And why
"Uncle" Kohn then? Because he was a character legends are made of,
like Uncle Vanya, the "little father" of Russian folktales, or the Uncle
Sam of Americano-imperialisto-capitalistic tales.

He really was not lucky, the uncle Kohn. He had prepared his passage for a long time. He paid the guide, sold all his possessions—not
for money, since the Hungarian forint had no value on the other side
of the border, but for diamonds. Before the war he had been a jeweler, a small jeweler not earning any more than was necessary for him
and his family, just what they needed to live on. He had kept his contacts, knew all the networks, the circuits—even though the war had
destroyed his contacts and hurt his networks, he had still been able
to manage putting together a small stock of diamonds in exchange
for almost all his possessions. When his shop was taken over by the
Communist state, he had to work there as a simple sales clerk. Kohn
had no family (bereft of family since 1945, since Auschwitz, whence he
had come back alone), no ties. One dictatorship, that of the Nazis, had
been enough for him. He figured that another, particularly so close
in time, that of the Comrades, was one too many, and if he could do
without it, well. . . . Kohn *bácsi* had always been on the wrong side. A
Hungarian in Romanian Transylvania, a Jew in Hitler's realm, a capi-
talist shop owner in Stalin's realm. . . . He needed a break. And then,
the things the Hungarians did to him and let be done to him and his
family and to his fellow Jews during the war didn't give him any in-
centive to stay in that country—in spite of the love, the sincere love,
he had felt for Hungary—before. Before it . . .

Old Kohn wasn't old; at fifty-five he could still make a new life for himself, find work again, and who knows, perhaps even a spouse. He wanted to go to the US, where his distant cousin Eugene lived and who would have been, along with the little stash of diamonds hidden on his person, his stepping stone into a new life.

He really had no luck. After the guide, a peasant from a border village who knew perfectly the territory, had him cross a river, make his way through the underground passages of an abandoned mine, through the barbed wire fences, then through the famous no-man's-land between East and West, Kohn had only a few hundred meters left to reach the streetlights of an Austrian village. He could already see the shadows behind the curtains of the lit windows whose inhabitants hadn't gone to sleep yet.

But all of a sudden, wham! Hearing footsteps behind him, then a dog's noisy panting, he rolls down into a ditch filled with ice water (a no-man's-ditch) where he curls up and awaits—fate. Fate comes to him in the form of a sublieutenant of the Hungarian border patrol who orders him at the top of his voice to come out of his hole. His choice of words is refined and clean, as is the custom in

—armies in general,

—the Hungarian army in particular,

—and in comparable circumstances.

Kohn *bácsi* has to retravel his earlier trajectory, but in the inverse direction, still on foot, still in the most total of silence, but this time solidly accompanied and with his hands bound, walking again for hours through the no-man's-furrows petrified by the frost. The only sound is the crunching of the soldiers' boots. Once back in the village, the village from whence he had left with the guide, he is brought to the officers' headquarters, which is overheated by a coal-burning stove and where the officers are smoking and drinking *pálinka*.

"Kohn *bácsi*," asks a commanding officer, full of himself and in a snickering mood, a mood created by the drinks, the heat, the lateness of the night, and the sight of the dangerous class enemy that they have just captured. Playing the important leader in front of his comrades, he asks: "Kohn *bácsi*, what got into you that you wanted to flee? Why did you want to leave our People's Republic? What's your problem?

What's not working? You came back from Auschwitz, alive! Miracle! You find a country in peace. Again miracle! You find your apartment again—a new miracle! And to spare you the suffering of loneliness, the Party, who sees everything and takes care of everyone, settled in your apartment four other tenants, good peasants come to town to work and who are keeping you company. We gave you work in line with your expertise, to you who were not even supposed to be alive! And instead of being grateful for your fate, or rather to the Party to whom you owe all this, what do you do? You try to leave the country, at night, illegally. Kohn *bácsi*, can you tell us why you did this?"

Old Kohn first thinks about his little pouch of diamonds hidden in his undershirt and realizes that once out of prison he would not have anything to live on. Then he scratches his head and says: "There's a rumor in Budapest that all blonds are to be hanged."

An astounded silence greets this statement. "What an ignominious calumny! Are there no limits to the nuisance the enemies of our democratic party are creating. And even if ? Kohn *bácsi*, you're pulling our leg! You're not even blond! You have lost almost all your hair and the remaining ones are dark brown!"

"I know," replies Kohn, "but until I succeed in proving it . . ."

21

Two Geopolitical Lessons

FIRST LESSON

When my friend Georges Banu gave me a small globe made of Murano crystal and told me this joke, I wondered whether it was linked to an epoch, a place, or a political situation. In fact, in spite of the date and the circumstances, this story is eternal—and it is its timelessness, its exemplarity, that give it its depth and darkness.

We are in Romania in 1991, the year when the Soviet Union fell apart. The Berlin Wall fell two years previously. The Communist regimes fell one after the other. This is also happening in Romania, where people can finally travel freely, go where they like. Low-cost flights aren't around yet, they have to pay full price, but no matter. Anyone who can afford it and fancies it can get on a plane.

Kohnescu, for instance: for a long time he has felt like a prisoner of the hundred thousand walls of his country, locked into its hermetic borders. He has some money saved up, not hard currency, oh no. Even though in 1991 it was no longer forbidden and no longer dangerous. It wasn't too long ago that you could have lost your life if that was the whim of a court. No, he has some lei, just enough to treat himself to a short stay abroad.

So our man is very happy as his imagination's eyes are filled with images of unknown seas and mountains robed in blue mist. Kohnescu goes early in the morning to a travel agency. At the time, these agencies were still official and state owned, though private travel agents were to soon make their appearance. He waits in line like a good citizen, usually one hour, in line, as usual, as everywhere, to obtain or buy anything. While the political regime has changed, the structures have not. Ah, there will come a day when one will regret the good old companionable lines, regret the lack of equality in the face of empty store displays. . . . And it will be too late: instinctive consumerism, excessive digitalization, and institutionalization will have beaten conviviality.

It's finally Kohnescu's turn. A young woman in full makeup, mascara, lipstick, fake eyelashes of a length totally unknown during Ceauşescu regime, jacket tailored very tight, showing a generous bosom to advantage, blond-colored hair (we are only describing what was visible above the countertop)—the young lady had switched regime with a flick of the wrist. . . . Kohnescu is tickled pink by it.

"Miss, I would like to take a trip."

"Of course, Mister Kohnescu." (How did she know our friend's name? Everybody knew him. Even those who didn't know him knew him. You've figured it out a long time ago: he was not a being of flesh and blood, but a symbol. The part for the whole. Kohnescu is Kohn, uncle Kohn; he's quite simply, unavoidably, you and me.) "Where do you want to go?"

Silence.

"Well, hm, it's a bit silly, hm, I must look ridiculous. I didn't give any thought to it. I was so happy to go that I didn't even think . . ."

The young woman has no time to chat. People in the line are getting impatient. "Here, Mr. Kohnescu—why don't you sit at that table with the globe of the earth on it. Take your time, give it some thought, and choose. With our travel agency you can go anywhere you fancy. When you have decided, I'll take care of you right away. You won't need to wait in line again."

Kohnescu sits down and studies the globe. The Earth is round. He makes it rotate around its slanted axes. It's a beautiful globe, with blue the dominant color. Kohnescu likes blue. Let's see, where will I go? Should I leave it to chance, close my eyes, and point a finger somewhere? No, that's no good. First thought: here on the shore of this little inland blue sea: Israel. Bad idea. He couldn't go there just for a few days. It's *his* country; and then, he has relatives there, he would have to visit them and thus couldn't do anything else, couldn't visit the country. And then, there's war there. Frankly, Kohnescu has had more than enough problems these last few years, last few decades. . . . All his life, from the time he was born, even these last centuries. Now he would like a bit of a rest. Travel, relaxation. No, Israel will be for another time. That country, *his* country, requires a long trip, an in-depth one. Right now it should be a first contact with the world, the taste for travel, traveling for its own sake. This big chunk, the United States, paradise on earth, the promised land. But it's much too big. And there too, so many problems! So many different people, insecurity. . . . And then, it's too expensive. No, Kohnescu has had too many problems lately and not enough dollars. Here, up there, the immense Russia, the countries of the former Soviet Union. Thanks but no thanks! I've had enough. I'm fed up with the Soviets—and also with the Chinese. And all the former Communist countries, Hungary, Bulgaria, and all the rest, absolutely not. In twenty years maybe.

The young woman raises her eyes and her voice from the other side of her counter: "So Mr. Kohnescu, did you find an itinerary to your taste?"

"I'm getting there, Miss; it's a bit slow. It's difficult for me, but I'm getting there."

"You know, if I had money, I would go to the countries up north. In Scandinavia, up there on the globe near the polar area. They say that the people there are great, friendly, it's not crowded at all, and nature is amazing. At any rate, different from here."

"Brrr," says Kohnescu. "How horrible! I can't stand the cold. And then I heard that these Scandinavians are heavy drinkers. No, I'm absolutely not going to start with northern countries. Well, let's look again at this globe. Here's India. Oh, no, all this poverty, people who starve to death right in the street—not for me."

Kohnescu keeps on twirling the globe, then stops it at random.

"Germany! No way, never. What with all that they've done to us. No and no. Nor Austria. In England it's raining. Arab countries: excluded; they wouldn't let me in anyway. They don't let Jews enter."

He plays with the globe, makes it turn, stops it, looks at the name of a country, makes a face, turns it again, randomly stops it again. . . .

The young woman calls him from her desk: "What's going on, Mr. Kohnescu? I'm surprised at you. Can't you decide? The world is so big and beautiful! And you haven't seen any of it yet! Why don't you go to the Caribbean, or the Antilles, or Polynesia, or an island in an ocean? I'll find you a good deal on a plane ticket or a ship—that's even better! A long, beautiful trip all the way to the ocean!"

"Of course, Miss, let's see, of course! Coconut trees, blue lagoons, *vahines*, a true dream. Gentle breezes, the Marquesas Islands—I read about them. A great French painter, Paul Gauguin, lived there. Ah yes, the dream? But I'm sure to be bored to death. Besides Gauguin died there. And this stupid tourism where you only see the sea and the palm trees and where all the difficulties, all of the harsh reality faced by the local people, are hidden—unemployment and poverty and alcoholism and violence . . . but we do know they exist . . . no thanks!"

Kohnescu has now been petting the globe for almost an hour. And suddenly, as if waking from a bad dream, he exclaims to the travel agent: "Say Miss, would you happen to have another globe?"

SECOND LESSON

I don't want to separate this story from the preceding one. They both mean exactly the same thing. This time our hero will be called Ledig instead of Kohnescu, and we will travel back in time by thirty years, or perhaps even forty.

We are at the beginning of the fifties. It's the time of Anna Pauker, a minister of the first Romanian Communist government. Mrs. Pauker was Jewish and it was rumored that she was the mistress of the great Communist leader Maurice Thorez (with whom she even had a child, but this is only gossip and I know nothing about it, I didn't do any research, I'm just repeating what I've been told without checking, so someone better not sue me for slander, I would deny everything, I would say that . . . I would say that this is only gossip and I'm just repeating what I've been told without checking, I even would deny having said what I'm in the process of saying, I would say that I am not the author of this short story, it's not me, Comrade Commissar

... and I'll still end up in the Gulag, or if lucky in the Lubyanka or Lefortovo prisons).[19]

Anna Pauker was a Communist and a Jew. She let Jews go to Israel, a unique case in the history of the people's democracies. (How did she end up? Very old in her bed?) Ledig took advantage of this and packed his bag and flew to *Eretz Yisra'el*, the land, the country of Israel. He was a Hungarian Jew of Transylvania, and he felt that in the new world coming to Romania, the two adjectives—Jew and Hungarian—were not going to be assets in everyday life. He wasn't very happy about leaving, because he was born here, as were his father, his grandfather, his great-great-grandfather, and he knew the intensity of every wind, the shape of every cloud, the smells, the history, the taste of food, the ways of thinking, of behaving, of living. He was not attracted to the unknown, to adventure. And yet, alerted by an infinite number of small clues, he became convinced that he had to leave, that he had to abandon all that.

Thus for the first time in his life he took a plane and a few hours later found himself in this country that wasn't that of his parents, that is Transylvania, but that of his distant ancestors—presumed ancestors—but the thought suffices, for would an in-depth study of genealogical reality change anything?

Once landed, he was taken care of. An *ulpan* to learn Hebrew, an apartment, right away a job—he was a furrier—money to help him settle, and mostly, not a single anti-Semitic word, gesture, or thought. Ledig was spoiled rotten in Israel, *wie Gott in Frankreich*, "like God in France." (So, can you explain this saying to me? In the country of the Dreyfus affair, in that of Monsieur Lavalbousquetpaponlepenraymondbarre[20] and of Madame Everymanjack. Karin tells me it came from Henrich Heine, yes, from Heinrich Heine, to be pronounced "hey-n," as in French, because the unfortunate Heine to be happy in France had to first convert to Catholicism while still in Germany . . .)

19. Actually it was a false rumor. I had dinner the other night with a historian preparing a well-documented biography of Maurice Thorez, and she denied the whole story.
20. [The author is turning a string of French fascists and extreme right wingers into one person. The separate names are: Laval, Bousquet, Papon, Le Pen, Raymond Barre. — TRANS.]

After a year of happiness, Ledig went to the Romanian embassy to ask permission to return to Transylvania. Well, of course, the authorization was granted! What a triumph! What a slap in the face of capitalism, on the face of Zionism! Romanian newspapers wrote about it, Ledig, the Romanian hero of socialism, was interviewed on the radio. Why did you come back? Weren't you happy?

No, he wasn't happy. Why not?—no response from Ledig.

Job, apartment, money, in short everything. He was immediately given everything from the Romanian government he had made so happy.

Thirteen or fourteen months after his return, Ledig goes to the department in charge of granting authorization to emigrate. He wants to return to Israel. Or anywhere, he doesn't care.

There's general consternation in the office.

"But, Comrade Ledig, that's no longer possible! You must be kidding! We're going to get angry, it's not a circus here. First you ask permission to leave. You are given a passport right away. That's so very rare, even exceptional, in our country, as you are quite aware. It's thanks to . . . it's because you are . . . well, let's not dwell on that. After a year, you ask to come back. We are generous and conciliatory: we give you permission to come back and you are helped to reintegrate into society with all means available. And now, you want to leave again. Tell us, Comrade Ledig, where are you happy, where do you feel fine, safe in this world?"

Ledig doesn't need to give any thought to his answer. He exclaims without a hint of hesitation, as if he had expected the question: "On the plane!"

22

In Someone Else's Shoes

According to Contes populaires juifs d'Europe orientale²¹ (Paris: José Corti, 2004), the origin, or rather the principle, of stories featuring a very powerful king, that is power itself, and a simple Jew goes back to Alexander the Great and can be found in the Talmud.

It happened during the retreat in Russia. The great Napoleon was flee-ing the big Russian winter that had vanquished him, just as it was to vanquish Hitler. (Apparently, the big Russian winter is in the habit of vanquishing foreign dictators. Too bad that it is powerless against local ones.) Napoleon was fleeing from General December, who was more tenacious, harsher, more resistant, more pitiless, and also more unpredictable than all the field marshals of the empire. (I don't know about you; I only know you from afar, and according to folk wisdom, all tastes can be found in nature. As for me, I am among those who have little taste for heaven-sent men, whom peoples, or rather court-iers, and then historians, called and still call Great, Victorious, In-corruptible, Guide, *Führer*, *Conducator*, Supreme Leader, *Generalismo*, *Duce*, *Dux*, *Caudillo*, Helmsman, *Lider maximo*, *Raïs*, etc., etc., and more etc. After their bloody reigns, these Fathers of the fatherland left and will always leave their country bone dry and their peoples as miserable or worse than before. The Peters, Catherines, the Fredericks, Louises, Benitos, Philippes, Iossif Vissarionovitches, Hitlers, Fidels . . . they don't like me. It's one more time a matter of *shmates*, material. Given the material they are made of and the textile the twentieth century has used to weave me, they cannot like me, and unhappily for them,

---

21. ["Jewish Folktales of Eastern Europe" — TRANS.]

the feeling is mutual. While they brought their people that part of the dream and the symbols that we all need, I cannot forget the price of this dream and these symbols. So, long live the Swiss government, its annual president, and its seven almost anonymous federal council members!).

And so the Great Emmmmperor (Damn! Atten-hut!), the master of Europe, and his *Grande armée* were miserably fleeing the cold, hunger, the towns and villages on fire, the Russian mujiks in rags armed with pitchforks, the partisans. They were fleeing fear itself.

The former *caporal* (a rank he had already forgotten), the former islander with his Corsican accent (he was ashamed of it), the son of an obscure and little-known noble family (a family he took very good care of), having gotten lost (on foot? on horseback? The *Encyclopaedia Britannica* is silent on this matter), having lost his entourage and his army, sought refuge all alone in the miserable hovel of a miserable Jewish violinist, Jewish and Russian, Russian but Jewish, Jewish but Russian.

"Jew, the partisans are after me—hide me or they'll kill me. You will be rewarded, I promise."

Napoleon didn't need to introduce himself. First, the *Encyclopaedia Britannica* specifies that Napoleon spoke Yiddish with a Corsican accent. Then engravings, anatomical drawings, and simple printed images had popularized his silhouette, his portliness, his tricorn hat, his white pants, his frock coat, the gesture so often repeated in front of a mirror of hiding his hand between two buttons of his vest. The Jew didn't expect for a moment that he would get a reward, particularly from an emperor in flight. Nonetheless, his religion taught him to be compassionate and to help those in need, without counting and thinking. Which is what he did. He quickly had the Frenchman come in, and had him lie down in his own marriage bed: the emperor with all his clothes on, with his boots, his overcoat, his tricorn hat. And with all his decorations and medals. His many decorations. Great cross, star, ribbon, sash, epaulette, pin, eagle, chain, distinctions and orders, assigned, offered, conferred, presented, bestowed by heads of armies and of governments, other emperors, kings, princes, popes: from the Catholic Apostolic and Roman religion, but also from the religion of betrayers, full of themselves, greedy popes lusting for temporal power, liars, lewd, thieves, weasel-faced—in alphabetical order). The emperor was wearing his bling-bling on his knee, around his neck, cross-wise, pinned to his uniform, in a buttonhole, sewed on his jacket, dangling from a ribbon. In his pants.

And now he was about to shit his pants from fear, but, wham! he finds himself suddenly in bed, under three eiderdowns, underneath comforters, blankets, sheets, Jewish goose feathers. And who would have believed it, the Russian winter victorious over emperors, a winter so different from a Corsican one. A real winter, minus twenty-five degrees, colder than a witch's teats, with snow several yards deep. We are two hundred *verstes* from Moscow, three thousand kilometers from Ajaccio. On another planet, that of Russian snow. It is top-grade snow, made in Russia, not imported, no need.

The emperor of the French is thus hidden in the violinist Yankel's bed. He isn't moving, barely breathing. He's trembling, fear-stricken.

He's right to be scared stiff, the emperor of the Frenchies. The partisans are tracking him. And here they are. They break down the door, push the Jew and his family against the wall, all the while insulting them (eighty years later, they were to undertake heroical pogroms), and engage in a systematic search of the house. This doesn't take long—the dwelling is not very big, we are not at the Rothschilds', not all Jews are wealthy, quite the contrary in the shtetls of the time. They don't find anyone.

The partisans leave empty-handed, proffering catcalls and spitting out insults, a number of threats and multiple warnings. Before leaving, while the others are already in the courtyard, their leader sits on the edge of the bed to adjust his boots. The bed moans and resists—it is in the habit of bearing two bodies.

Yankel waits for the noise to die down before telling Napoleon to get out of the bed.

The great reorganizer of peoples, of nations, of borders, and of the laws of the world first gives a small terrified look to the room to reassure himself, then he very carefully slips one leg out of the bed, then another, then his ass, and finally the rest of the emperor of the French appears in all his puny splendor.

He stands up to his full imposing height. (They say that without Napoleon, the inferiority complex of short people would be intolerable. Wrong! Today, photo-cinematographico-digital techniques make it possible to magnify even the smallest of *des grands de ce monde*! Well, just their images, the only thing that matters.)

In the meanwhile the imperial entourage has found the imperial tracks, and ragged soldiers of the Great Imperial Army enter the house.

Napoleon orders them to wait outside.

"Jew," the emperor who is again imperial deigns to address him. "You've saved my life. I promised you a reward. Ask me three things and your wishes will be granted."

Because a promise is a promise, even one made to a Jew.

Yankel scratches his head. He doesn't need anything. Peace, inner and outer peace. And that, this genius strategist couldn't give him. He is not capable of it. On the contrary. He only brings rape, misery, famine, death, the whole thing prettily wrapped up in a Parisian gift wrap, with the latest fashion in ribbons and bows.

"I don't want for anything"—and at that point he doesn't know how to address Napoleon: Sire? Mister? Mister Emperor? Your Majesty?

"Take time to think," responded Napoleon, flabbergasted that this miserable musician, living in this hovel with his family dressed in rags, claims to not need anything. "Take advantage of this opportunity. You don't see kings in your village every day."

"It's true," thinks Yankel. "Let us thank the Eternal for it."

Napoleon insists. Then Yankel's wife steps forward to ask that the French soldiers waiting outside redo the roof of the house. Rain, wind, and snow have for a long time seeped into the house.

As soon as it was said, it was done. Napoleon goes out in the yard and gives some brief orders.

"While you are thinking about your second wish, my men shall repair your roof. So what is this second wish?"

"I don't have a second wish. I no longer have any wish. Everything is fine. I am happy. God gives me help when I need it."

Napoleon was thinking that this Jew was really too stupid. Anyone would have jumped at the opportunity to ask a large sum of money or a title of nobility or a position at the court or a domain in France with a castle or a . . . whatever, something important. And they say that Jews are smart!

However, he can't stand being contradicted. He made a promise to this man—this promise must be kept. It will not be said in the Russian countryside that the emperor of the French is a liar.

"All right" says Yankel suddenly. "A French violinist settled some time ago in the neighboring town of Ivanograd. Before his arrival the people of Ivanograd, and not only the Jews, would call on me for bar mitzvahs, marriages, and other holidays. Now that he is here, I've lost half of my customers. Rich Jews feel it's more chic to have a French violinist perform at their wedding than a Jewish one. And yet this French musician, this Mister Vontobel, is not even French. He is Swiss. And he plays very badly. And then he doesn't know our own music. He only plays French music, lacking in rhythm, energy, attractiveness, and very boring. I heard him once; nobody was able to dance to his tunes. Since you want to help me, move this Mister Vontobel away, to another town, far from me and one without a violinist so I could get my customers back."

"No problem. Think of it as done."

And Napoleon calls his aide-de-camp. He gives him his orders, in imperial French.

"Now for the third and last wish. And hurry up. I've already wasted too much time with you."

In the meanwhile the roof of the house is done. It is resplendent, brand-new. Better than it has ever been. Instead of the thatch of the poor, a miracle, a solidly built roof of real slate shingles. Yankel was only to find out later, at his expense and very bitterly, that the soldiers had taken the shingles from the church to fix his roof. But that is another story.

Yankel feels completely gratified. He thinks, "I was right to let this Frenchman, this Bonaparte, come into my house."

And he is ready with his third wish. It isn't a wish. It's the famous Jewish need to understand everything.

"Listen, my third wish is that you answer a question so as to satisfy my curiosity. What did you feel, you the hero of heroes who makes tremble the Universe, peoples, kings, and princes, you the most powerful man next to our tsar, what did you feel when the leader of the partisans sat on the bed in which you were hidden, so close to you he could have touched you?"

"Enough!" sputters Napoleon. "Not only you are dumb, idiotic, stupid for not taking advantage of my promise, to not seize the opportunity to get out of your misery, your filth, your ignorance, but in addition, you are impertinent. You are forgetting whom you are addressing. I am Napoleon the First, in person!"

And the emperor again calls his aide. "Seize this rebellious Jew and put him in front of the firing squad! That's an order."

Before Yankel is even able to say "no" or "why," soldiers grab him, drag him into the yard, and tie him to a tree. His wife and children throw themselves at the feet of Emperor Napoleon I, in person, kiss the legs of the soldiers, beg and cry, but nothing doing. In spite or because of its defeat, the army honors its traditions of cruelty and inhumanity.

And here is Yankel, our poor Jewish violinist tied up to his favorite tree, the one under which he likes to take a nap, in his own yard. He cries, sheds tears, and implores his God, the Eternal God of the Jews. We can hear the commanding officer yell out: "Aim!"

A that moment, Napoleon signals with his hand to stop the execution. "Untie him," he says. He goes to the musician, who is on the ground gripped by an agony of fear. "So here is your third wish. I answered your question. Now you know how I felt."

He Who Hunts . . .

I am once again borrowing a story from the remarkable Contes populaires juifs d'Europe orientale *cited earlier. I am transforming it, reworking, denaturing, actualizing, and politicizing it. As I am appropriating it, I thus become part of a long brotherly and sisterly line made up of all those who held it in their hands, who held it between their lips, and reworked and actualized it in their own time.*

Kohn—oh my God, it's him again, after all that's happened to him (and here I don't dare imagine what else will happen to him in my tales and in his life)—is sent to the West, to Paris, charged, on behalf of a big Hungarian state-owned company, with negotiating a big deal. In fact, it was his thorough knowledge of Yiddish that, in his superiors' eyes, made him the perfect representative to lead successful negotiations in France. This was of course entirely theoretical knowledge, as Hungarian Jews did not speak Yiddish, something that Kohn's superiors weren't aware of. We are in the 1950s. One had no right to travel and hold foreign currency, but Kohn is on an official trip. He will be in possession of foreign currency. He is charged with selling the famous Hungarian snails to a French company that will transform them into the famous snails from Burgundy. And with the money earned, Kohn is to negotiate the purchase of a nuclear plant. The means of bringing these disgusting crawling animals to the snail eaters (no Hungarian would ever swallow such a gross, slimy thing) had been the topic for several meetings and much discussion. Being totally ignorant of the ins and outs of snail transportation, they had even contemplated the idea of having them travel on foot (on snail's feet, that is) with the help of a powerful lure, for instance, a very exciting and ultraspeedy female that would lead all the males in her wake. (This somewhat an-thropomorphic solution had to be abandoned when Comrade Füge-falevél remarked that the snails would have no particular reason to follow a female snail because there was no such thing, as snails are hermaphrodites. The comrade Fügefalevél had studied Buryat litera-ture, of which he had become the best and sole specialist in Hungary. However, since they couldn't find him a position fitting his scholar-ship, he had been assigned to head the export section of the firm Im-port/out-Export/in, specializing in nonferrous metals. And since the socialist republic of the Buryats was a part of the great Soviet Union, and moreover since Comrade Fügefalevél had very cleverly married a Buryat woman, his opinions were acted on as if they were orders. So no one dared ask him the meaning of the word "hermaphrodite"). Fi-nally, and for obscure reasons, it was decided to give up on the trans-portation of Hungarian snails and instead to buy Romanian snails. Even though these were far from being as good as Hungarian ones and much more difficult to collect, they were prepackaged and already loaded on a truck that would go directly from Bucharest to Paris. (The sequel of the deal, even though it's not part of our story, would have involved the judicial system, if Moscow hadn't intervened. In fact, the French paid the Romanians directly, as they had been able to ne-gotiate very advantageous terms. This is yet another instance where the Hungarians have managed to lose all the wars in which they were involved while the Romanians managed to always, at the last minute, find themselves on the side of the winners. It was only after payment that the employees of the French export-import firm, Burgundysnail, opened the crates and became enraged at finding that the Romanians, wanting to please the Hungarians and show their gratitude for hav-ing provided them with such a good deal, had printed with great dif-ficulty but successfully on the shell of each snail: "Made in Romania for Hungary," which made it difficult to sell the little beasts under the label "Burgundy snails.")

I'm coming back to Kohn, since he is the hero not only of this story but also one of the main heroes of this book, and we are more inter-ested in him than snails and nuclear plants.

Shortly before his departure for Paris, the secretary of the Par-

ty section, the comrade Egészhülye, calls him to his office. Comrade
Egészhülye is of very humble social origin, thus valuable for the regime for ideological reasons that, even more than his abilities, made
it possible for him to accede to this important position: that is, he had
never left Hungary, didn't speak any foreign languages, and was completely ignorant of everything. In spite of this, he explains at length to
Kohn how he should behave in France's capital, Berlin, how to inter-
act with French comrades and particularly the class enemies he'll be
forced to meet. His explanations last . . . and last. He does know, however, that all Westerners speak English, the imperialists' language, in
business dealings; German, the idiom of militarists' seeking revenge,
in political discussions; and French in brothels, which he specifically
advises Kohn to avoid. All he says about the West comes from the
courses he has been lucky enough and privileged to take at the Party
postgraduate school.

Kohn is feeling uncomfortable. All the increasingly confused and
confusing explications are turning into a worrisome diarrhea of words.
Comrade Egészhülye has never shined through his oratory talents,
and at any rate he has never shined through anything, except through
his origins, but something is obviously troubling him. Kohn detects
some sort of uneasiness, something unsaid. What is happening? Do
they want to cancel his trip? Or worse? A speedy bit of a trial because
. . . no matter because of what? Is there a cog missing in the wheel of
a prefabricated trial, and he would be it? The pretext would be found
as they went along: sabotage (the word was in fashion), illegal possession of foreign currency, spying. . . . The possibilities were endless.

"All right" says Kohn, hoping to precipitate a denouement, it's
time I get going, Comrade Secretary of the Party. I don't want to steal
any more of your precious time. I'll come to greet you before my departure, and of course I will provide you with a detailed account of
my negotiations as soon as I return. I'll do all that . . ."

The Party secretary of the Section for Enterprise interrupts him.
He is drenched in sweat. "Well, Kohn, you see . . ."

Oh shoot! thinks Kohn. This is the moment that the Goons of the
ÁVO, the political police, will jump out of the private bathroom of the
party secretary to arrest me. Kohn too is drenched in sweat.

"You see, Kohn, my wife has been nagging me for years to get me to buy her a *belound*. Even though our socialist state and the Hungarian workers are getting wealthier by the day, and the word 'penury' now belongs to the past of cosmopolitico-fascist capitalism, one can't find any *belound* in Hungary. Since my numerous duties here prevent me from traveling, I have never been able to make her this gift. You are a trustworthy man, recognized as such by Party authorities, so much so that your nomination to a position of great responsibilities with a substantial raise awaits you upon your return. And then, it is well known that Jews are intelligent and very resourceful and they stick together."

There's a great silence. So now we're getting to the point; it must be a trial for Zionist activities.

"I would like that with the help of, hm, I mean your compatriots, your friends, in short your relatives, your fellows, your, your—" Comrade Egészhülye is at a loss as to how to get out of the ideologico-religioso-ethnico-linguistico quagmire he has gotten himself stuck in—"what I mean is that with the help of other Jews you would buy me a *belound* in France."

There's a new silence, one horribly long, sweaty, squirmy.

"I have, hm—this is horrible for a Party secretary—a few dollars set aside." But this is awful, thinks Kohn. He's going to end up in front of a firing squad and now myself, because I know about it, I've become his accomplice and I'll get life. At the same time, I do have a hold on him! Kohn doesn't know if he should be exulting or dying of fright. "This is of course just between us," Egészhülye lamentably continues. "All this is strictly between us, Comrade Kohn, between us people holding high positions and conscious of the class struggle and the threat posed to us by the inhumane world of capitalism."

"Of course," says a relieved Kohn.

"I've saved fifty dollars to make this gift to my wife. Here they are."

"Comrade Egészhülye," responds Kohn without a second of hesitation and without touching the dollars, "you'd never get a quality *belound* for fifty dollars. What am I saying, quality! No *belound* at all. Even not a used one. Nothing. I'm telling you, I know about this. I'll gladly help you out with this. No problem. The small danger to bring the *belound* across the border, to give acceptable explanations to the custom officials, this danger, small but real, I'll risk it gladly so you can make the lady Comrade Egészhülye happy. I understand what this *belound* represents for you, and for the comrade your wife. However, please be reasonable. Don't ask me to do the impossible. A *belound* for fifty dollars, no way! I must be clear on this. If you can't put more money in it, I can't be your man."

"So, how much would be needed?"

"Comrade Egészhülye, a quality *belound* worthy of the name starts at two hundred dollars. It's the lowest price. Thanks to my contacts and particularly thanks to my vast knowledge of the *belound* market, I could try to get one for a hundred. Below that, don't even think about it. And it would be better to give me one hundred and fifty. Just in case I come across a possibly unique opportunity to buy the *belound* of your dreams. You wouldn't want to miss this opportunity on account of a measly fifty dollars."

Egészhülye is sweating blood. To admit that he has hidden foreign currency is already very painful—and very dangerous. But it's done; Kohn is now his accomplice, and thus he won't say anything. But from there to admit that he owns more than fifty dollars, even one hundred and fifty!

They engage in earnest discussion. The deal is a big one, the stake is important, the protagonists are tough. Each of the two adversaries wants the deal to conclude, so they end up toward the middle, around one hundred and twenty dollars. Egészhülye, with the speed of lightening, pulls out a great number of five-dollars bills from his pocket, and Kohn then slips them even faster into his own. No receipt, no written traces, that's an absolute no-no!

Kohn takes his leave. Another few words about the goal of the trip, its political and strategic import, the fraternal collaboration between Hungary and Romania in the domain of snails, an essential domain in the building of a solid and durable peace in the world, then a few final comments on the relation of the Hungarian snail industry and nuclear power.

Suddenly already at the door, Kohn turns around: "One more thing. Comrade Egészhülye, I forgot to ask you, what is a *belound*?"

The World of Business

Joey is the one who told me this story. It comes from his parents, American Jews, or from their ancestors who hailed from Europe. This is thus an old and well-traveled story.

Goldberg comes across Berg in San Francisco in the middle of a street. Was it by accident, or did fate organize this meeting? After all, there's no end to what fate is capable of.

They exchange the appropriate greetings. It's been a long time since they've seen each other, since so and so's birthday, that's too bad, how are you.

"I'm not doing so well," says Berg without further ado. "We're getting a divorce, me and Lisa."

"What? After so many years of living together? But come quick, let's get on the sidewalk or we're going to get run over."

"What can you do, that's the way it is. As to getting run over, too bad. I don't give a damn."

"No way!" exclaims a laughing Goldberg

His good mood is not contagious.

"Anyway," says Berg, his voice depressed, his eyes tired, his back bent, "in fact we should have accepted doing this a long time ago. We were still hoping that it would work, you know how it is, laziness, you get used to a situation even if you're unhappy. You postpone the decision for yet another day. And then you're afraid to take such an important decision which. ... This is so depressing. You have only one life, you're given only one hand, you try to play intelligently. You start to live, I mean live with a woman—why? Just to be able to have sex whenever you feel like it, without having to try to pick up somebody every day? It's not only that. Well, it's that and much of that, but that's not all. It's also a quest to not be alone, To not have to struggle on your own, to not be alone when ill, when you die. To share with someone your ideas, the landscapes that you are seeing and liking, just about everything . . . I would almost say, but I'm afraid to use big words, to give meaning to your life."

Berg couldn't stop talking. He visibly felt the need to explain himself. Perhaps to forgive himself? To find excuses?

Goldberg interrupts him. "But that's too bad. What's the problem? At the beginning when I met you two, you were so much in love with each other. Who is cheating on whom?"

"Oh, that's not the case at all. There is no major adultery or casual one-night stands. Far from it. You're right, it was a great love. Then life took over. There were difficulties, children, illnesses, problems with work, money, in short, life. We were unable to resolve these problems together. It was not a case of everyone for themselves but of one against the other. We were unable to reach an agreement. It was a constant power struggle. Who's making the decisions. Who's in charge. Horrible. Well, enough talking about me. And you, how are you doing?"

"I've experienced everything you're describing," answered Goldberg. "We, Sarah and I, we also went through this. Daily yelling at each other. Even in front of the kids! Word for word, the same as you two: who was going to have the last word. Who was making the decision, who was prevailing. That's what happens when two strong personalities live under the same roof."

Berg's became very interested. "And then?"

"We solved the problem. Nowadays we are living in peace and harmony. We each contributed to the solution."

Berg: "Do tell. This is fascinating."

Goldberg: "Yes, it's pretty simple, you see. One day after a huge fight followed by a huge silence, Sarah made the first step. I was very moved. She proposed we go to a restaurant so that we could talk about our problems in neutral territory, away from our apartment, a dwelling with which we were too familiar, with too many connotations, as she says in her psychotherapist's language, too charged with negative electricity and energy. So, we went out to dinner and Sarah told me: 'Listen Jack, that's enough. We love each other, we have always been there for each other, we are not going to just wait for our lives to turn into hell and for us to start hating each other. I don't want this war anymore.'"

"OK," says Berg, "and then?"

"I liked the idea. I completely agreed with her. She made me an offer. She said: 'Let's lay out our issues on the table. Let's share the tasks, divide the decisions.' And thus we reached an acceptable compromise."

"Tell me, I can't wait to hear your method," begs Berg.

"It's so simple and ingenious," responds Goldberg. We divided the issues of familial life into two groups. Minor issues requiring minor decisions and major issues requiring major decisions. My wife Sarah, seeking peace and harmony, agreed to deal with secondary matters and to make the small decisions, while I would make the important ones."

Berg is amazed. "That's wonderful, that's ingenious, and that saved your relationship. I'm running off to talk to Lisa about it. Perhaps it's not too late. How lucky that I bumped into you today! So tell me, what are the small and what are the big decisions? Give me some examples."

"It's not complicated, I'm telling you again," answers Goldberg. "The small decisions pertain to the small matters of everyday life that don't require long debates or deep reflection, and which are, to tell the truth without me playing at being macho, the women's domain."

"For instance?"

"For instance, should we go out tonight or not, and if we go out what are we going to do, movie, restaurant, or something else, and if we are going to the movie theater, which film should we see, and even more insignificant questions: the country in which we will live, whether it will be in the countryside or in town, and if in town, in which one, and will we buy or rent our apartment, how many children should we have, which school the children should attend, where will we go on our vacations, who will our friends be and who will we avoid—well you get the idea—and many other pretty lightweight matters. So it's my wife who decides these things. Alone. I don't meddle in them."

Berg is struck dumb. "Hm, I understand. Hm, it's pretty clear. So tell me, then what are the big decisions?"

"Big decisions are those requiring reflection, deep thinking, culture, readings, serious study. The kind of study required by big issues, important matters. Let me give you, in no special order, a few among those I'm presently concerned with: the problem of Iran nuclear program, the quicksand that is Iraq, the painful question of the poverty of the underprivileged classes, racism, the Chinese commercial danger, Russia's growing power, and, what else . . . , AIDS, Kosovo. Or again the rise of Islamism. And let's not forget above all the future of our planet, global warming, etc. You see the type of issues. Well, these are the real vital issues, the true great concerns, and it's up to me to resolve them. Alone as well. And that's a lot of work, believe me!"

25

Games of Chance

I already knew this one when I was a kid in Budapest. This anecdote is loved by all those, that is Jews, still dreaming of a harmonious world. There's no need to mention that this family joke (which I got from my family) dates from before World War II. Because after the war, priests and rabbis no longer socialized with each other, and mostly there were no longer any rabbis in Austrian villages.

In an Austrian village, one not very small but rather the size of a burg, before the First World War, during the years of the "time of peace" or "the world of peace," as they said during the Belle Epoque,[22] the Catholic priest, the pastor, and the rabbi were getting along very well. The large majority of the inhabitants were Catholic, however there was also a sizeable Jewish minority and a few Protestants. We can't say that the three men of the cloth were actually friends, because if they had been, twentieth-century Austrian history would have unfolded differently—at any rate for the Jews. Nonetheless, they did appreciate each other, took pleasure in getting together, in conversing with each other. All three were cultured, even erudite. The priest was open to the world and to new ideas; the pastor read Hebrew and was very familiar with the Tanakh;[23] as to the rabbi, a Hasidic Jew, he had unbounded curiosity and joie de vivre.

The three priests would meet often, at least once per week, to debate religious matters and points of dogma, to discuss the ways taken by the country and the world, to talk politics, to exchange gossip, to

22. I'll spare you from my favorite pet peeve of the time of *k. und k.*, imperial and royal. For more in-depth elaboration, see the short story "Fish Heads," in *Two Jews on a Train*.
23. That is, the Hebrew bible.

drink a bit of schnaps and to . . . play cards. Forgive them, oh Lord. Pleasures on this earthly plane are so few. Even though all three of them were persuaded of the immortality of the soul and the resurrection of the bodies, even though all believed that men and women in Heaven would get their reward for their earthly suffering and that they would sing in joy and happiness seated at the right of the Lord, they refused to despise the pleasures of this world, those that can be enjoyed during their brief passage on it. They liked normal pleasures, without being slave to them (the rabbi and the pastor were moreover married!).

Well yes, they did play cards now and then. Innocently. The stakes were minor, a few *groschen*. It was true that their religions forbade games of chance. Why is that? Since God is at the origin of everything and He is omniscient, there's no such thing as chance! Him, the One Above, knows ahead of time, even for all eternity, who is going to win and who is going to lose. He even knows by how much, because it's He who organized it this way.

That day they were playing poker. A friendly game while conversing. They had the same accent; they spoke the same dialect. It was in October, the sky was cloudy, at times it was raining, and at times you could feel the last weak rays of the dying summer sun. It was in October, and instead of the usual schnaps, our men of God were drinking new wine and eating nuts. Delicious. ("Delicious are the new wine and nuts" is a verse from the great poet Georg Trakl. Even though Trakl was not Jewish, I am hanging on to his only relationship with our history, the fact that he was Austrian, to speak of him. Read him and you'll thank me for it.)

Suddenly there's a mighty thunderbolt. Then another one, and lightning and more lightning as it had never been seen. And then the rain suddenly starts to fall, in a frenzy, furiously, drops as big as stones. Heavy, cold, threatening.

The priests are not afraid. Although . . . such cosmic force, such rare violence. We are in Central Europe and not in the tropics, for heaven's sake! Our priests are believers, but not superstitious. Thus they keep on playing and conversing.

And suddenly—I am myself shaking as I'm telling the story, as I too feel the exception, the never-seen, the Mystical Terror—the sky opens up, a heretofore unbeknownst light floods the world, and they can hear a Voice, a Voice that they feel they've known forever and that terrifies and crushes them, a voice coming from everywhere and that floods and envelops them, and that they don't hear with their ears but with all of their being.

And the Voice speaks to the Catholic priest while the card game has gone hiding as if by itself in the drawer under the table. "My son, did you play cards?"

"No Lord, I did not play cards. How could you think this about Your servant? We have come together here as men of the church to debate religious matters. The Immaculate Conception, my colleagues are questioning it. They come up with pseudo-scientific arguments, but I'm fighting them because I am inhabited by the true faith. Likewise . . ."

God doesn't listen anymore. He knows, he sees the human soul. He addresses the pastor. "Did you play cards?"

The shepherd of the Protestants protests, overcoming his fear: "No, Lord. We were talking about "sufficient grace" and "efficacious grace." I have just reread Calvin's *Christian Instruction*, and each time I'm reading it, it sheds light on my path with a new . . ."

And the rabbi too, also terrified, hears the word of the Eternal. Moses was the last man whom God directly addressed. And now . . . "And you, did you play poker?"

The rabbi raises his face toward the ceiling representing Heaven, opens up his two hands, palms turned upward, and says in a strong and almost reassured voice: "Eli, by myself ?"

26

The Emigrant

I have to admit that this story is an orphan. From whence did I get it? Who entrusted me with it? Where did I read it? It is one of those timeless tales that are circulating, in disguise, in depth, in despair . . .

Shlomo, a young Lithuanian Jew from Vilnius, has decided to emigrate to the US (in reality they said: "to America"). He has been saving for a long time; and now he has enough money to be able to leave. We are at the very beginning of the twentieth century. In spite of the fact that Vilnius was then referred to as the Jerusalem of the East, Shlomo isn't happy. One could write many dissertations on happiness. I already cited Camus's "happiness is a gift." Shlomo has been deprived of this gift, but he is very talented when it came to misfortune, pessimism, the too-bad, for the negative, for being crushed in darkness, for depression, for despair. Why should he care for the famous Talmudic school of his city, the large size of its Jewish population, the many young girls he could have married? He just wants to leave.

After numerous attempts to change profession, fiancée, life, he decides to change country—even continent. You might as well say, world. America doesn't resemble anything, has nothing in common with Lithuania, and Vilnius certainly not with New York. It is a different world.

And yet, he is hesitant. He's afraid. In fact he's afraid of everything: of the ship, the trip, the unknown, of his ignorance of the language, of the fact that he doesn't know anyone on the other side of the ocean. He's indeed scared of changing worlds.

He keeps complaining, imaginary complaints, that is, to whoever is ready to listen to him. But no one wants to listen and they are all making fun of him.

"You're so lucky to be able to leave!" the people keep on saying. "You're free like a bird, like the wind: no family, no wife, no children. You possess nothing, you can climb aboard with your hands in your pocket."

One day he bumps into his old buddy Itzik in the street. He opens up to him, to him too. Itzik, along with the whole town, has been aware for a long time of Shlomo's wish to emigrate, and he totally approves of it. What have you got to lose? Etc. He sings to him the tune that Shlomo already knows by heart: You're free like a bird, the ship, hands in his pockets. There are also surprising variants. He knows them all. Neither wife nor child; his parents are dead—so? What is he waiting for to climb on a spiffy ship that is neighing and bucking like a horse! So ship, go! Open a path through the waves toward the promised land! (You must have noticed that our two fellows are not very pious; otherwise they would never dare call another country besides Israel "the promised land"). Listen to me: a land without anti-Semitism, where everyone is equal and one can be happy—while here . . .

Itzik is the opposite to Shlomo. He thinks positively, only looks at the sun, even in winter, even at night.

"What are you afraid of, Shlomo?" asks Itzik. "Think about it, there are two possibilities: either they let you get on board ship in spite of your sickly complexion or not. If they don't accept you, it's all for the best, your wishes are granted, you can return home. If you climb on board, there are two possibilities: either there will be a storm or there won't be. If there is no storm, everything will be all right. If there is a storm, there are two possibilities: either you'll get horribly seasick or you won't. If you get seasick there are two possibilities: either you are so seasick that you can't even get out of the ship on Ellis Island, or you overcome your illness. If you vomit all the time, that is good, they'll send you back to Lithuania as you were wishing. If you overcome your seasickness, or pretend to overcome it, and they allow you to disembark, there are two possibilities: either you'll find a well-paying job in New York or you won't find any. If you find one, all will be all right. If you do find work, but horrible work, there are two possibilities: either you'll succeed in quitting or you won't. If you can quit it, all will be all right. If you don't find another one and you have to keep that job to feed yourself and survive, there are two possibilities: either you'll get sick or you won't. If you don't get sick, all will be all right. If you collapse with exhaustion, illness, or misfortune, there are two possibilities: either you'll get well or not. If, thanks to your strong constitution, you succeed in regaining your health, then all will be all right. If you keep on being bedridden because this job is so depressing or so inhumane and hard, there are two possibilities: either you'll survive or you'll die. If you survive, all will be all right. If you die, there are two possibilities: either these Americans give you a Jewish funeral or they won't. If they bury you in accordance with the religion and the rites of our people, all will be all right. In order to avoid getting buried any which way and place, in any old cemetery with goy rituals, you have to request, as soon as you get off the ship, that you want to be buried, immediately upon your arrival, in a Jewish cemetery and according to the Jewish religion—and all will be all right!"

27

Of Money, Still

I'm telling you three stories about money and Jews. I could tell you two hundred, two hundred and fifty, a thousand, fill you up with them, to the point of making you a misanthrope. But not an anti-Semite—surely not. Is it necessary to tell you that Jews are neither more nor less interested in money than the rest of humankind, and that only our enemies make us to be greedy and cheap folks? Do you want me to cite names from France itself, names of characters deeply rooted in the French soil but who are not Jews nor Armenians nor Scottish, nor this and that, and who don't need any lesson in matters of shameless swindling, gross greed, crooked financial dealings? Haven't you heard of La Farce de maître Pathelin?[24] And Molière's character constantly complaining about the money owed? And did you read Balzac? And the rest? And daily newspapers? And what about the shady dealings of one or other minister of state, president, or such and such captain of industry, Monsieur Y, Monsieur de X? Sometimes though rarely, and not often enough by a long shot, they go to jail. But they come out! And start again! Well, then. I'll tell you my jokes anyway, because they are funny.

I realize as I'm speaking that all three of them, though picked by chance, have something in common: they play on the virtual. On the "as if," on the denial of reality.

ONE

Kohn is in misery. Well, he's so miserable I don't want to call him Kohn. My, our, Kohn never fell into that sort of poverty, so dark, close to beggary, that of the state of a chronic *schnorrer*. I'd rather call him

---

24. ["The Farce of Master Pierre Pathelin," a famous French fifteenth-century comedy featuring a number of picturesquely dishonest characters. — TRANS.]

Himmelreich. Are you comfortable with that? It means "Heaven's empire." He engages in strange deals; he buys something here to resell it there; he borrows here to repay nowhere. Everyone knows this in his small town, everyone fears him, everyone avoids him.

It's market day. Himmelreich wanders among the kosher butchers' stalls and those of herring, sprats, cloth, brushes, millinery merchants, around mountains of onions piled on the ground on a blanket. He wanders among all the merchants who have come there to earn what they need to live till the next market day. He takes on the allure of an important man as he looks at everything, asks for prices with the haughtiness of a connoisseur, handles merchandise like an expert, squeezes like a specialist, caresses with sensuality, feels, tastes, and spits like a gourmet . . . and tastes and swallows like someone who's very hungry. He tries everything but doesn't buy anything. The male merchants keep their eyes on his hands, the peasant women on his pockets.

Suddenly he bumps into Taschenlehr, a wealthy jeweler who is also a usurer in his off hours. Himmelreich lets out a sincere exclamation of joy. "Taschenlehr! I was just looking for you! I need you. I am onto a hot deal. A shipment from Warsaw, unbelievable, for a ridiculously low price. Lend me the money to buy the lot, and in addition to paying you back, I'll also give you twenty-five percent of the profit. Is that OK with you?"

"How much do you need?"

Himmelreich states his price: two hundred zlotys.

"I can't lend you two hundred zlotys. That's too much. It's not worth it."

"A hundred and fifty would also do. I'll negotiate the price of the merchandise. And I'm keeping my offer: twenty-five percent of the profits will be for you."

"No," says Taschenlehr, a man of few words. "It's still too much. I don't have the sum on me. And I want fifty percent of the profits."

Himmelreich produces nervous sighs and coughs. "All right for a hundred zlotys. It's just because it's you. You'll thank me. And I also agree to the fifty percent of the profits."

"That's not good either. You're still asking too much. One hundred zlotys are way too much. And, while we are at it, I want sixty percent of the profits. After all, I'm the one paying."

"But I can't possibly buy all this merchandise for less! The seller would think I'm crazy—or worse, a neophyte who doesn't know anything about business. So tell me how much you want to pay me, and I'll try to figure out something. Eighty five?"

The discussion is long; it takes forever. The sum keeps on getting lower. The two protagonists are already down to ten zlotys without having reached an agreement. The arguments fly back and forth. The two men are sweating blood.

Himmelreich throws in the towel. "Let's stop this negotiation. We are both wasting our time. How much do you want to lend me?" he asks, tired, exhausted, discouraged.

"Nothing, I don't want to lend you anything."

"So why," exclaims Himmelreich, "why did you go through all this discussion? Why did you ask me how much I needed? Why did you then make me keep on lowering the sum? Since you knew from the start that you weren't going to lend me anything?"

Taschenlehr gives him a speedy reply: "It was to lose as little as possible. I knew you weren't going to give me back my money."

TWO

As it often happens in Jewish stories, there is a variant depending on countries, on storytellers—I'm not calling them authors, because they are always unknown. We are here in the domain of oral folk literature.

Here in this story, Himmelreich again wanders through the market. This time he is accompanied by his cousin, younger, more inexperienced. They come across Taschenlehr, the rich jeweler whose stall is elegant even in the market. Himmelreich happily exclaims: "Taschenlehr, I was looking for you! My son is going to have his bar mitzvah and I want to give him a watch. Yours are the most beautiful ones. Show me your wonders."

Taschenlehr is happy to comply. He's a clever merchant, yet not indifferent to flattery. No one is safe from self-satisfaction; this particularly applies to craftsmen. You only need to praise the fruit of their labor, and you'll see! Caution just flies out the window. You might remember the verse: "Know that every flatterer lives at the expense of the one who listens to him."[25]

"Let's see then," says Himmelreich, his eyes smiling with pleasure, with wonderment. There are Longines, Omegas, Rolexes, IWC Schaffhausens, Vacheron & Constantins, Patek Philippes . . . and particularly Doxas! Oh Doxa, a Swiss brand totally unknown in Switzerland, but thanks to clever marketing—or thanks to chance?—it is extremely well known and prized in all of Eastern and Central Europe.

"What are you looking for," asks Taschenlehr, "A pocket or a wristwatch?"

"A wristwatch, of course. Don't you have children yourself? My son is thirteen. He doesn't even have a pocket in his pants to put a watch in."

"So give him the most magnificent I have, my Doxa in 18 carat gold. Anyway, I assume that he's not going to wear it at school, and that you'll display it in your curio cabinet in the living room?"

Himmelreich agrees. Of course, it's out of the question to risk a watch in a schoolyard rumble.

He picks up each watch, weighs it in his hand, listens to it, winds it, asks Taschenlehr to set it, inquires about the warranty. . . . In short, he gains time before tackling the main scene, the opening of act 2: the price.

"This one, how much would you charge me?"

Then begins the long, endless, complicated negotiations. They go from one watch to another, agree on one hundred, but then for this price you get this one, no, I want the Doxa at the price of the Breitling, you must be kidding, you don't know the worth of a Breitling, Count Potocki wears a Breitling he bought from me, then let's go for a hundred, and the Schaffhausen, you don't know what you're talking about, you know nothing about watches, it's not a watch for a

25. [From book 1 of the *Fables* by Jean de La Fontaine, the very famous poem "The Crow and the Fox." — TRANS.]

kid, it's Count Branicki who buys Schaffhausens for his children, and not for a hundred zlotys, if you please, at five hundred zlotys a piece, yes, etc., etc. Do you really want me to give you all the details of this oratorical, commercial, sportive, heroic, quasi vital joust? And yet the prices do get lower, insensibly for Taschenlehr, considerably for Himmelreich—or the opposite. They each complain, groan, swear, pray, yell, abjure, injure, disparage, beg, threaten, raise their arms to heaven, beat their chests, call the cousin as witness, address neighboring stalls, stop passersby, abandon the discussion, begin to busy themselves with other things, go away, come back, start again with a much lower price—or much higher, according to the protagonist. It's great sport and spectacle. And Himmelreich very cleverly makes sure that even though he is putting the merchandise down, to never put it down too much, and he keeps on praising the merchant, making him important, flattering him, lulling to sleep his predator-negotiator instinct under a blanket of compliments on his watchmaking talent, on his refined taste, on his worldliness, and as an international businessmen.

So they must come to a conclusion, just as in tragedies, just as in comedies, haggling has its rules, its duration, its laws. The market Aristotle whose name, birth and death dates, and nationality we don't know, laid them out in his famous treatise.

The two actors, the two protagonists, come to an agreement in the midst of complaining and fuming. The time has finally come. Himmelreich requests a gift box, then a festive wrapping and a silk ribbon, then leaves, after promising to pay Taschenlehr at the end of the month.

One hundred yards away, his cousin turns to him and asks: "I don't understand you, cousin. Why did you negotiate so hard and so long? Since you weren't going to pay him anyway, and you are perfectly aware that you'll never pay him. You don't have a dime."

Himmelreich replies to his cousin as a teacher would to a pupil. He even raises his hand and his index finger. "You have to understand. It's true that I won't pay him, mmm, at least not in the very near future. It's also true that at the moment my cash flow is a bit on the short side. But I like this merchant, and moreover he's one of my wife's cousins.

It was thus my duty to obtain the lowest possible price, in order to make sure that he would lose as little as possible."

THREE

And they leave the market, Himmelreich and his cousin. It's lunchtime and they're hungry. They've spent all morning in the middle of latkes, piragis, strudels (with poppy seeds, or apples, or nuts . . . me too, I'm getting hungry) and other Polish, Russian, Hungarian, Austrian foods without buying anything—and now hunger pangs are affecting them.

However, as you just read, they don't have a dime. And suddenly, to their happiness and great unhappiness, they are passing in front of the open door of a restaurant very near the market. Why happiness? Because from the restaurant emanates delicious aromas of cabbage, goose fat, roasted geese, onions, freshly baked bread, the whole mixed, interlaced, each smell embedded in the others even while remaining perfectly individualized and identifiable. And why unhappiness? For the very same reasons! Because these delicious aromas announce, reveal, succulent dishes, dishes that are out of reach to Himmelreich and his cousin. They must content themselves with stopping, closing their eyes, opening their nostrils, shrinking their stomachs, pumping full those brain cells devoted to imagination—and thus to enjoy and suffer in silence.

Their silence is broken by the arrival of the restaurant owner, who rushes out of his kitchen. It just happens that he's a cousin of Taschenlehr whom they both know well.

"What are you doing here? Go away or pay me for smelling my food. After all, these are my dishes, my cooking, my food, which you are enjoying, and since it's only the smell, I'll make you a lower price. But you have to either pay or go away. This is not a soup kitchen."

Himmelreich and his cousin leave, angry, frustrated, desperate.

But life, no matter what they say, is unpredictable. Particularly for us Jews. We have seen in the twentieth century enormous fortunes fly away, be stolen, disappear (and often their owners flew away and disappeared at the same time), as well as the opposite: the multimillionaire Guggenheim, fleeing from Russia, a poor tailor, with eight or nine children; the Hungarian refugee Soros, who became king of New York financiers. . . . So, Himmelreich made his fortune. Right there, in his own town, without being forced to go away to America. How? It would be too long to tell. He did it almost honestly and not always and not necessarily dishonestly. So, he's rich—that's should be sufficient for the story. The ways to acquire wealth are many and tortuous. So one evening he invites his cousin, the same one, though ten years older, to dinner. This in the famous restaurant near the market from which ten years previously such delicious and expensive smells emanated.

The restaurant has come up in the world. From good it has become famous, excellent, fashionable, luxurious, and incredibly expensive.

Himmelreich and his cousin take off their astrakhan coats and sit down at a table they reserved over the phone. The waiter gives them the menu: golden, printed in three languages and six colors, extra large—this to impress customers and prepare them for the exorbitant prices listed therein. A second waiter brings them the wine menu.

They chose their appetizers . . . and then, no, I'm not going to describe their meal. Saliva is already accumulating in my mouth from the description of the market food. If I now have to list the dishes, my favorite ones, those of this Central European cuisine that I'll love till the end of my days, I'll faint. From pleasure rather than hunger—we no longer ever feel hunger, us, the haves of the West.

Himmelreich and his cousin pick the most refined and succulent dishes.

They choose and eat, and they drink. Champagne to begin with, then French wines, and after the coffee, cognac and cigars. They converse very pleasantly. And time passes. It's getting late. Himmelreich calls the waiter. "Your boss is Taschenlehr, right? Ask him to come to our table with the check. I want to pay it."

"Sir, you can pay me," replies the waiter.

Himmelreich wishes to pay the boss directly.

The customer is king. The boss comes to the table, the very one who's Taschenlehr's cousin, you remember him? He's obsequious. He's the same as ten years ago, but ten years older. He brings the bill which Himmelreich carefully studies. Then he approvingly moves his head up and down, pulls a large bill out of his wallet, takes it between his thumb and index finger, puts it near the restaurant owner's ear and rubs and crumples it so that it produces some sound. Then he puts the bill back in his wallet, puts his wallet back in the inside pocket of his jacket, and the two buddies stand up and walk in the direction of the cloakroom.

The owner, in a panic, follows them. Hesitating between politeness and worry, he calls them: "Hm, excuse me, you haven't paid . . ."

Himmelreich slowly turns toward the owner, puts his face right in front of his, looks him in the eyes, and says: "Listen to me. Ten years ago I was starving. You wanted to make me pay for the aromas that emanated from your food. Well, today, I pay for the food with the sound of money."

∗ ∗ ∗

Even though this is a very Jewish story, it is also already found in Rabelais, told by Panurge. Kohn bacsi would deduce that Rabelais was a Jew.

28

Of Us and Them, of Them and Us

I collected this story in a Parisian café during a dinner with Vilmo, a Hungarian
intellectual, cosmopolitan, brilliant, funny, and not even desperate, emigrant
from everywhere; and Danielle, a Parisian woman, pretty, funny, and in despair
for no other reason than the usual human ones . . .

Kohn, again. He's done some slightly shady deals, not shady enough
to make lots of money justify the risks he took, but too shady for me
to tell them to you, I, whose parents have only left me the recommendation of work and honesty.

Kohn finally can escape semipoverty, full poverty. He now has a
bit of money. Enough to be able finally to fulfill his dream, to reach
what he has waited for all these years, what he has aspired to so much:
elegance. To be well dressed, chic, fashionable, with spanking new
clothes, custom-made, custom-made just for him.

He goes to the best tailor in Budapest. And he orders what a *gavallér*[26] needs to have: several suits, gloves, neckties, a dozen shirts.
Then he buys hats: top hats, bowler hats, panama hats, boating hats.
He has lacquered shoes custom-made. And he also buys underpants,
handkerchiefs, socks along with the elastics to hold them up, wax
and brushes for his mustache, nets for his hair, new shaving accesso-
ries such as a brush, a straight-blade folding razor, a leather strap to
sharpen it, and finally an eau de cologne scented soap.

When everything is ready, one Sunday morning, Kohn gets up very
early. He chooses a light-colored suit, a flattering necktie, a pair of

26. [The word *gavallér* is a Hungarian transformation of the French *cavalier*. It means an
elegant, courteous, and well-bred man who knows how to court women. — TRANS.]

deer leather gloves the color of fresh butter, a top hat in gray silk har-
monizing with his suit. Picking out his clothes and getting dressed
takes hours. He goes out whistling a tune from Kálmán's "The Princess
Czardas." He's in a spring mode, sunny, all green, all in bloom for his
inaugurating his new clothes in the city park, which is also in spring
mode, sunny, all green, all in bloom. Young ladies are already there,
sunny, all in bloom, under their sun umbrellas, with their friends or
chaperones.[27] They strut and Kohn goes into peacock mode. They are
not the only ones there; there are children with their young and pretty
mommies (again? Enough, Kohn; it's not because it's spring that you
have to have such a one-track mind), soldiers and others in well-fit-
ting uniforms, bourgeois men arm in arm with bourgeois women
and their small dogs (yes, the small dogs carried in their arms) . . .
who else? Oh, yes, members of the supporting cast: the park guard,
the employee who picks up papers from the ground with his pointy
stick, several suspicious-looking individuals such as the unemployed,
wanderers, small crooks looking for opportunities, a few gendarmes.
To be in tune with the time we should call them by their nineteenth-
century appellation: coppers.

The cast is complete, all the actors accounted for. Kohn can begin
his triumphal walk.

Birds are singing. That's what they usually do in spring. They fly all
over the place and sing. There are lots of them, of all kinds and sizes;
however, their colors are fairly dull. We are in Hungary, in Central Europe, where the climate is continental. We are not on a Pacific island or
in a New Guinea forest, the destinations of bird-watchers one hundred
years hence to seek the flash of flamboyant, fabulous colors.

It is only noon, but there is an impressive number of park visitors.
It's the first beautiful Sunday of the year.

It is then that all of a sudden one of the many singing birds drops
an enormous turd on the shoulder of Kohn's splendid light-colored
brand-new suit. There is muted laughter from the young ladies, their
chaperones, the young and pretty mothers, the male and female bourgeois, and their offspring—who stop chasing their hoops to better

---

27. The Hungarian equivalent of a chaperone was in the nineteenth century (but who
knows, perhaps even today?) *gardedám*.

see—the soldiers, even the gendarmes. As for the thieves, no need to mention them . . . they are laughing very loudly, openly. Only the small dogs remain indifferent.

Then Kohn, after taking a look at his soiled, ruined suit, and, worse, realizing that he is ridiculed, lifts up his head more sad than angry, toward the bird, one of the many birds: "Seist di, far de goyim singst di!" ("See that? For goys you're singing!")

Literally, one should translate: "You see, for the goyim, singing you are!" May the one who can do better raise her or his hand.

29

The Negotiation

We started this book with Kohn, and we are going to end it with Grün—and with God. The three main characters of this book, and also of the Great Book of our lives, of the lives of the Jews. Grün, Kohn's clone, the basic Jew, at times dirt-poor schnorrer, and at times disszidens in a Communist country, at times very rich Westerner. Like all of us. And it is good, indispensable, to know that as long as we exist, from Grün to the Rothschilds, we can be one day poor schnorrers and the next, wealthy tycoons—and the opposite. Then the opposite again. Or somewhere in between . . . most often in between. And, though I'm thinking about them all the time, I'm not talking about the pyres of York, of Troyes, of the Venice ghettos of Medieval times and the Krakow ones of the twentieth century, and of the unnamable camps.

The story that follows is not a witz. I've read part of it, its opening play, in the Contes populaires juifs d'Europe orientale *already cited several times, and I invented the rest.*

One day, a king enacts a decree: all Jews must leave his kingdom before the end of the month.

There's consternation among the Jews. They don't understand this decision, which, moreover, they weren't expecting and which fell upon them like a bolt out of the blue. They have lived in this country for generations, as long as the other inhabitants. They are happy here, well at least as happy as you can be on this earth, as happy as the Lord allows. What was their fault, what have they done to merit this cruel punishment?

They all gather, in each village, in each town, in the synagogue and pray; they pray night and day, the men wearing their *thales* and their *tefilim*, the women with their tears and cries. The rabbis order a day of fasting just as at Yom Kippur so as to mollify the Eternal's anger, and they pray to Him to forgive them their sins. They send a delegation to the king, who at first refuses to see them, then has them told to wait because he's very busy, and finally, after days and days of anguished waiting, he sees them just to tell them dryly that there's no appealing his decision and that any Jews who haven't left by the end of the month will be executed on the public square and their possessions confiscated. Besides, to those members of the delegation who, behaving like true Jews, have asked for the reason for this inhumane decision, he answers that he is sovereign of his country by divine right and that he doesn't have to give them any explanation.

Jewish households are filled with tears and complaints. There is no longer any hope. Where can they go? They have always lived here; they don't know anything, anyone, elsewhere. They should be sending emissaries to other Jews in other countries, but time is running short.

Only Grün, the feebleminded, isn't crying. They all say that he's too dumb to understand what is happening, that we have to abandon our houses, our lands, our workshops, our studies, our shops, our temples, the places of our memories, trees and bushes, grasses and weeds, the flowers, the birds, and this sky which we know and which is the only one that we know.

Grün, the simpleminded, calmly answers: "First, it is Jewish destiny to leave. If we must leave, we must. Read our Book: since the destruction of the Temple, we have always been on the road. Nonetheless the question has to be asked: must we leave? And why? We have an alliance with the Eternal. He gave us the Torah. He gave it to us, I insist; He gave it and didn't lend it. I was surely there, though I don't remember it. This book of laws belongs to us. He gave it to us in token of our alliance with Him. This book of laws teaches us to be humane, kind, tolerant, and to have a good appetite. And justice. Justice! Why is God breaking His promise? We are His chosen people. He told this to Abraham, He told it to Moses. We married Him, we are His fiancée. Me, Grün, I'm God's fiancée. He entered into a contract with us, a marriage contract. We worship Him and only Him and no other god, we obey the *mitzvot*, the commandments He gave us, and we carry them on our shoulders like the ox carries its yoke. We celebrate all the holy days He gave us. In return, He owes us justice and protection. He wants to break the contract that we respect to a tee, while He, He rips it up and takes up the side of our enemies? How could He act in this way against us? I am a Jew and I don't agree. Because I am Jewish and the ox and the fiancée of God. I want for God to do away with this law; I want for God to force the king to annul it."

"Hey you, the ox and the fiancée, and what if He doesn't annul it?" asked the others.

"This would be very serious. It would mean that He broke the contract and that we can no longer trust Him. I would then put down my yoke; I would no longer carry it."

"And how will you convince the Holy One to make this iniquitous law change?"

"I want to summon Him. I want to discuss this with Him."

There's a terrified silence. What a sacrilege even coming from a nut!

"And why not discuss it with the king? After all it's he who proclaimed this law."

"The king, like everything, like the beasts in the field, the trees in the forest, and the little birds singing in the trees, is God's instrument. He can do no other than to obey His will. When a shingle falls from the roof of a house on my head, I don't start to discuss the situation with the shingle, nor the roof, but with the owner of the house and the architect who built it. And that goes for this decree. It is He who created this king, the producer of the decree I want to discuss. I don't want to waste my time haggling with the roof or with the house."

Some of the people who are listening to Grün are surprised at the apparent rightness of his talk, while others are terrified to hear spoken out loud the idea of summoning the Supreme Architect, God. No human being has had a conversation with God since Moses! Only a madman could even think such a thing!

Grün is holding fast to his plan. He wants to have a personal discussion with God.

"What have we got to lose? In any case we'll have to take the road to exile, again, the road of misfortune with only misfortune for a companion and at the end of which only misfortune awaits us. God is just. God is good and God loves us. We are His people. This has to be a mistake."

"A mistake! You're really crazy. God cannot make mistakes! You're mad and a miscreant! But He'll forgive you. You are not able to understand what you are speaking about."

"So He must have fallen asleep, and wham! The king takes advantage! Or He has another purpose. We have the right to know what that purpose is. He can't just play this way with His people. Do we have to accept each misfortune, each blow, each wound by bowing our heads and without uttering one word or asking any questions? Is it all right for Him to piss on us? So then what is the use of living? We might as well not be born or die right away. He has plans for us, so we must obey His will? He couldn't want our misfortune."

"And what if it's a punishment?"

"So let Him punish the guilty, but not me, Grün, who never did anything wrong in my life, except fall asleep at the synagogue. And He should not punish a whole people! And if we are all guilty, it's the human species that is guilty—and who created the human species? Would God create something completely bad from the very beginning? It's you who are the miscreants. You think God is bad!"

Terror spreads among his listeners. Instead of preparing to flee, people are gathering on the public squares, in the temples, in the houses, and discussing, arguing, about the words of a simpleminded, mentally retarded man. Nonetheless everyone is very shaken by Grün's reasoning. Some people are saying that madmen often utter the truth. Others think that a *dibbuk* is speaking through Grün's mouth. Some, forgetting his madness, address him as if he were someone important, and ask him how he plans to go about it . . .

"Let us all go to His house," Grün says, "summon Him, and demand that He listen and respond to us."

The discussion could have lasted days and days, probably forever, or at least till everybody would have been massacred by the king's soldiers, if Grün hadn't made the decision of going immediately to the synagogue and inviting all those who agreed to follow him.

No one wants to follow a madman, or rather no one dares enter the synagogue with him.

He thus goes alone to the house of prayer and closes the door behind him, since he was told that he has to talk alone with God.

Once in the house of God, his head entirely covered with his prayer shawl, his hands trembling, his eyes closed, Grün the feebleminded exclaims in a voice he doesn't recognize as his own: "Lord God, Almighty Eternal, why did You punish us this way? Answer me, I'm Grün, Your creature!"

A terrible silence ensues. All of Grün's body is trembling.

"Oh Sole God, Eternal, let us know what sins we have committed to merit such a punishment, or retract the edict. It is not right to punish us for a fault we did not commit or of which we are unaware. You made a covenant with us. We are doing all we can to respect each of its terms. We await the same thing from You."

Silence.

Then imperceptibly, barely audibly, the synagogue door opens.

Grün still awaits in silence, still shaking, his head still covered, his eyes closed.

Nothing more. Just the open door.

Grün comes out of the synagogue, hollow-eyed, his step shaky. The others make way and no one dares speak to him.

He takes up again his daily work, enveloped in total silence. He doesn't even talk to his family. He is the man who has talked with God. He can never again speak with human beings.

The others, terrified, prefer to insist on his madness. They keep on praying, lamenting. And they are packing, killing those animals they can't take along, getting lost in speculation about the responses of the Jews from the rest of the world, still hoping for help from abroad.

Grün keeps on working in his stall, in silence, forever.

After three days, the king's heralds proclaimed that their sovereign, in his magnanimousness and wisdom, has decided to annul the expulsion law.

∗ ∗ ∗

I am ending the present book, this book of witz that aims to be funny, joyful, with this story that is not conducive to laughter but whose optimism is to remain engraved in our hearts. Karin and I have just written a narrative of a horrible trip we made to Kaliningrad, the ex-Königsberg of the former Eastern Prussia, the cradle of my wife's family. It's a text of great, enormous sadness. And I ended my portion of it, in spite of my publisher's objections, with these words: "We sure are laughing!"

THE END
(of the stories)

AFTERWORD

I could, I really wanted to tell you, more of them. I have a long list of other stories, very beautiful ones, often very funny, with which one could spend long evenings—yet, you must be as tired as I am. One day, perhaps, God willing, as my grandmother Blanka used to say . . .

The stories you have just read only have meaning if they keep on living. I am thus taking the liberty of making a request: please, appropriate these jokes for yourself and tell them in turn. And the more you change them, the more you add your own sense of humor, your own moods to them, along with your knowledge, your life, the better they will be.